The Loves of Lakeside

Can't Fight the Feelings

The Loves of Lakeside

Can't Fight the Feelings

MIMI FRANCIS

4 Horsemen
Publications, Inc.

4 Horsemen Publications, Inc.
1497 Main St. Suite 169
Dunedin, FL 34698
4horsemenpublications.com
info@4horsemenpublications.com

Cover by Tony White
Typeset by Autumn Skye
Editor Blair Parke

Library of Congress Control Number: 2023932676

Print ISBN: 978-1-64450-829-9
Ebook ISBN: 978-1-64450-861-9
Audio ISBN: 978-1-64450-832-9

Dedication

*T*iana, this one is for you. Your unwavering support, smiling face, and love keeps me going; your off-the-wall insanity keeps me smiling; and your advice never fails to be on point. Thank you for pushing me to be better. I love you.

Table of Contents

Chapter 1

Natasha

"**N**ate!"

Natasha pounded on the thick wooden door, hard enough to make her hand ache. For a second, she wondered if she was in front of the wrong house; all of the homes in this area looked alike. It wasn't like she was thinking straight, either.

"Nate!"

She stepped back to check the house number, took a deep breath, counted to ten, and started pounding again with both fists.

"Nathaniel Boris Garin, open the goddamn door!" she screamed.

The door flew open so suddenly that she stumbled forward, landing on the hard wood floor of the small foyer on both knees with a startled "oof." Natasha's twin brother Nate stood at the door, wearing nothing but his boxers, his reddish-brown hair standing on end, and his blue eyes flashing. She'd always been jealous that Nate got their mother's deep blue eyes, while hers were gray like their father's.

"What the hell, Natasha?" he snapped. "Are you drunk?"

"Jesus, no!" She pushed herself to her feet and stalked past her brother, elbowing him in the gut as she passed him. "Why the hell would I be drunk? God, you're an insensitive asshole."

"Hey, you're the one beating the shit out of my door and barging into my house in the middle of the night!"

"Oh, god, why don't you just shut up?" Natasha shouted.

She entered the modest living room, dominated by a big screen TV and a sectional sofa. She dropped her backpack on the floor, threw herself on the sofa, put her hands over her face, and burst into tears. She'd been holding them back ever since she'd walked into her apartment and found her boyfriend, Brick, with that woman.

Natasha didn't know how she got to Nate's place; she remembered little after grabbing her backpack and storming out of the apartment she shared with Brick. It didn't surprise her that she ended up at Nate's house. Her brother was her rock, always there when she needed him. Going straight to his place for comfort was the only thing she could think to do.

Nate slammed the door shut, rested his head against it, and stared at the floor. "I repeat, what the hell, Tash? What are you doing here at two in the morning?"

Before she could answer, a door on the other side of the living room opened, and a giant of a man stepped out. Topping out at 6' 6", Mason, Nate's roommate and best friend, towered over both of them. Relief washed over her at the sight; Natasha hoped he'd be here. Her brother's best friend—her friend—would make everything better; he always did. Though it annoyed her that once again, Mason was witness to her bad taste in men.

"What is going on out here?" He pulled a shirt over his head then ran a hand through his shoulder length black hair, pushing it away from his face. He froze when he saw Natasha, and his eyes narrowed. "Why are you crying, Tasha?"

"Crying?" Nate vaulted over the back of the couch and landed beside her. "What happened?"

Natasha shook her head. "I don't want to talk about it." She hiccupped and wiped her nose with the back of her hand.

Nate scoffed. "You show up at our door at two in the morning, pounding loud enough to wake up the entire block, and you don't want to talk about it? I don't think so." He put his arm around Natasha and hugged her. "What did that asshole Brick do now?"

Natasha opened her mouth to tell her brother not to call her boyfriend an asshole, but instead, she lost it. She collapsed into her brother's arms, her head on his chest and tears pouring down her face. The story of finding her fiancé in their bed with another woman came out between her sobs and curses. Once it was all out, Natasha fell against the back of the couch, hiccupping sobs escaping her and with tears and snot all over her face. She was also bearing the hefty stares of one sympathetic friend and a pissed-off twin brother.

"I'm going to kill him," Nate growled. Once Natasha had the whole story out, Nate shot to his feet and paced back and forth in front of the couch, fists clenching and unclenching at his sides while his brow furrowed. Anger radiated off him in waves. "I am literally going to kill him."

"Nate—"

"When are you going to stop letting him treat you like crap?" her brother snapped. "When?"

Natasha sighed. "I don't *let* him treat me like crap. It just happens. And I don't want to have this discussion again."

"We won't have to if you tell me you're breaking up with him this time."

"He's my fiancé, Nate. I'm supposed to marry him." *Not like that's going to happen now.* The thought brought a fresh wave of tears. A reassuring hand settled on the small of her back, instantly soothing her. She glanced over her shoulder at Mason and gave him a grateful smile as her brother continued his tirade.

Nate rolled his eyes at her excuses. "He's your fiancé in name only. You've been engaged for almost a year, and you haven't set a date. He makes excuse after excuse to avoid making the commitment. Ever since he lost his job at the university, he's always drinking, he can't keep any other job, and he's making your life a living hell. And now, he cheated on you." Nate's voice got louder with every word. "What more does he need to do? How much shit is he going to put you through before you decide you've had enough? When are you going to figure out you deserve better?"

Natasha jumped to her feet. "Stop yelling at me!" she screamed. "I've had a terrible day!" She took a step toward her brother, the urge to slap his perfect face overwhelmed her.

Mason was on his feet in a second, stepping between them, with his arm going around Natasha's waist. He swung her off her feet, moving her away from her brother, and then put a hand on Nate's chest. "Alright, you two, that's enough. I think we've all had enough … excitement for one night. Why don't we get some sleep, and we'll pick this up in the morning?"

Nate glared at Natasha, slapped Mason's hand away, and stalked across the room. The slam of his bedroom door echoed through the small house.

"He's a little grumpy when he first wakes up, especially in the middle of the night," Mason said.

"I know." Natasha sighed. "I'm sorry, Mason. I shouldn't have come here. I didn't know where else to go. Shit, I didn't have anywhere else to go." Another bout of tears threatened, thickening the back of her throat and making it difficult to talk. She closed her eyes and rested her forehead against Mason's muscled chest as he pulled her into a hug.

"You're always welcome here, Tasha; you know that." Mason kissed the top of her head and released her. Afterward, he opened a small closet next to the bathroom door, pulled out some mismatched, faded sheets, and tossed them on the couch. "There's a blanket in the cupboard under the coffee table if you need it."

"Thanks, Mace," she mumbled. Her brother's best friend was the consummate good guy. He was unbelievably nice, one of those guys who did stuff for other people without being asked, the guy who stepped up to help when no one else would. He was the good guy, to a fault. Whenever she needed him, he was there; sometimes she hated that about him, especially when she could only find the losers to date.

Mason smiled at her. "Get some sleep, Tasha. You can fight with Nate in the morning." He was almost to his room when he turned back to look at her. "Nate's right, you know. You deserve better."

———

The smell of coffee pulled Natasha from a restless sleep the next morning. She propped herself up on her elbows, squinting as the light hit her eyes. Across the room, thanks to the open floor plan of the small house, she could see Mason in the kitchen. He must have been out running because he wore basketball shorts, a zip-up hoodie with no shirt, and running shoes. There were a pair of earbuds in his ears, and his long, black hair was pulled into a tight bun at the back of his head. He had an odd look on his face as he pulled coffee cups from the dishwasher.

Natasha sat up and rubbed her gritty, puffy eyes. Her head pounded and her throat was raw from the emotional night. She shoved herself off the couch, wrapped one of the sheets around her waist, snatched her jeans off the floor, and stumbled into the bathroom to change. Ten minutes later, she emerged to find a cup of hot coffee sitting on the scuffed and marred coffee table, along with three sugar packets, a plastic spoon, and two of those little creamer cups. Mason sat on the couch, remote in his hand, while the other sheet and the blanket she'd used were bunched up beside him to form a barrier between them when she sat down.

"Thanks for the coffee."

"You're welcome." He glanced at her and smiled before he put the TV on some sports program, propped his feet on the table, and sipped his coffee.

Natasha poured the sugar packets and creamer in her coffee, stirring it with a plastic spoon. It was funny that Mason knew exactly how she took her coffee; she wasn't even sure if Brick knew how she took her coffee. Mason also knew she wasn't a morning person, and he knew when she needed to talk and when she didn't want to talk.

Natasha had known Mason since elementary school. He had lived three doors down from her family growing up and went to the same elementary school, junior high, and high school. She had known him when he was seventy-five pounds soaking wet, with unruly, black hair that stuck up in every direction, through junior high when he'd been awkward around girls, gangly, and unsure what to do with his changing body, and through high school, when he suddenly shot up in height and weight the summer between junior and senior year. The only person who knew Mason better than her was her brother.

Even though Mason was Nate's best friend, she and Mason had always been close. Mason was almost as important to Natasha as her brother was; he was the guy she could turn to when Nate became irrational or too brotherly. He kept both of them grounded and stood by them, no matter what. She hated that they'd grown apart since high school because of her stupid decisions, though they were still good friends.

Mason looked at her out of the corner of his eye. "Are you okay? Did you get any sleep?"

Natasha chortled, sounding a little like a sick chicken. "Yeah, I guess so. As good as one can sleep when their world is turned upside down, and they have nothing other than the clothes on their back."

She'd run out of her apartment with nothing but her backpack—no clothes, no makeup, no money. It was uncomfortable sleeping in her tank top and underwear. She'd tossed and turned on the narrow couch, wondering if Mason would venture out and see her with little clothes on. Just the thought that he'd seen her sprawled across the couch in her underwear made heat rise in her chest and across her cheeks.

She shook off the thought and gave Mason a tight smile. "I am sorry you had to get in between Nate and me last night. We tend to get a little emotional."

Mason laughed. "It's not like it's the first time I've broken up a fight between you two. I'm sure it won't be the last." A grin spread across his face. He turned to face her, his arm propped on the back of the couch. "Do you remember that time in third grade when he switched lunches on you?"

Natasha thought back over the multitude of fights over the years between her and her twin brother. She giggled as the image of the three of them in grade school materialized in her head. Mason had weighed maybe forty pounds and looked like a string bean, she looked like Pippi Longstocking with her long red braids, and Nate had a bowl haircut she still teased him about.

"Oh my god, yes! He wanted my peanut butter-and-jelly sandwich, right? So, he switched our lunch bags at home. I got his bologna sandwich. I hate bologna. Hate it."

Mason chuckled. "I remember you chasing him around the lunchroom. You almost caught him the third time around."

Natasha nodded. "That's right, I did! Except you jumped in front of me and shoved your lunch into my hands. It was a peanut butter-and-jelly sandwich."

Mason nodded. "And Nate lived to see another day." He cleared his throat. "You know, I hate bologna, too."

"Really? I didn't know that." She narrowed her eyes as she looked at Mason. "If I remember correctly, you ate Nate's lunch that day."

He shrugged. "Yeah, I did."

Nate's bedroom door flew open, interrupting their conversation. Her brother emerged, fully clothed this time, and made a beeline for his sister's side. He pushed the pile of blankets to the floor and sat down, elbowing Mason out of the way. Nate took Natasha's hands and held them tightly in his.

"I'm sorry I yelled, Tash," he said.

Natasha smiled and squeezed his hands; it was time for the inevitable apology. "It's okay. I get it. You're my big brother."

"By eight minutes," he reminded her.

"And you worry about me." Natasha glanced at Mason over her brother's shoulder. He was pretending not to listen. "You're right. Both you and Mason." She dragged in a deep breath. "I deserve better. So, I'm done. I'm leaving Brick, for good this time."

Nate released her hands and jumped to his feet, pumping his fist in the air. "Yes! It's about time. I'll help you move out. Both Mace and I will. In fact, we'll go tonight and get your stuff. I'll get Trista to watch the bar." He did an obnoxious little dance. "Wait? Are you … are you going to move back to Great Falls? Live with Mom and Dad?"

The thought of living with her parents made her head hurt. She couldn't move home, not after living on her own for the last five years. Moving back into her childhood bedroom under the constant scrutiny of her overbearing parents was not appealing. Her entire life was here in Lakeside, more than four hours from her childhood home. She didn't want to go back to Great Falls, except she didn't have anywhere else to go.

"Well, shit."

Nate, always attuned to her feelings, knew what she was thinking. He kneeled in front of her. "You can stay here as long as you need to until you're back on your feet. Right, Mason?" He smacked his friend on the leg for confirmation.

Mason gave Natasha and Nate a weird look, mumbled something that sounded like "yeah" under his breath, and then he catapulted himself off the couch and into the bathroom. The shower could be heard turning on a few seconds later.

As soon as the door closed behind Mason, a huge grin spread across Nate's face, and he laughed. "This is gonna be fun."

Chapter 2

Mason

Nate might have been his best friend, but sometimes he seemed more like Mason's worst enemy. Letting Natasha stay with them for one night, maybe two, was one thing, but inviting her to *live* with them was something completely different. Nate was completely aware of Mason's crush on Natasha and the fact that he had been head over heels in love with his best friend's sister for years. Now he'd gone and invited the woman who held Mason's heart in her hands to live with them for some time.

I will not survive this.

Mason turned the shower to cold, trying to get the memory of the petite redhead sleeping on their couch out of his head. Every time he closed his eyes, he could see the sheet tangled around Natasha's muscular legs: her panties stark white against her tanned skin, her tank top pushed up beneath her breasts, and her hand splayed across her stomach. After seeing that, he had to run an extra two miles to calm down.

Fortunately, by the time he got home from his run, she'd rolled over and pulled the sheet over herself. Of course, five minutes later, Natasha stood up, stretched—revealing more skin—then dragged the sheet around herself, and went into the bathroom. That was another sight that would fuel his fantasies for a while.

Shivering from the cold Montana water pouring down on him, Mason shut off the shower, grabbed the towel from the bar, and wiped off just enough of himself to keep from dripping on the hardwood floors. He wrapped the towel around his waist, threw open the bathroom door, and came face to face with Natasha. Startled, he took a step back, causing the corner of the towel to slip out of his hands and leaving him almost completely exposed, except for his dick, which was barely covered by the towel.

Natasha stared at him for at least thirty seconds, her mouth hanging open and her entire face so red, it matched her hair. Once she realized she was staring at Mason—or, more accurately, staring at Mason's dick—she spun around and, for good measure, put her hands over her eyes.

"Oh my god, Mace," she snapped. "Would you put some clothes on, please?"

"Shit," Mason mumbled. He scrambled to rearrange the towel around his waist. Once he'd secured it, he clutched it so tightly, his knuckles ached. "Sorry, Tash." He pushed past her, dove into his room, and kicked the door closed.

Yeah, this is gonna be fun.

—

Mason drove to work with the truck windows rolled down and the radio blaring country music. He thought it might help get Natasha out of his head, but it didn't work.

He was at the photography studio before anyone else, which didn't surprise him. Harry Ward, the owner of the studio, lost his enthusiasm for his job after his wife passed away six months ago. Mason suspected Mr. Ward would soon close up shop and move down to Missoula to be closer to his grandkids, so Mason figured it was time to look for a new job.

"Maybe Nate will hire me," he mumbled, as he unlocked the door and stepped inside the dark studio.

It wouldn't be the first time he'd worked for a Garin, which was Nate's last name. Back in high school, he'd worked for Nate's father, cleaning and detailing cars at Mr. Garin's three car dealerships in town. During college, both he and Nate worked at the Time Out Bar and Grill; when Mr. Garin helped his son purchase the popular hangout, Mason stayed on, working for Nate. The Garins were such a huge part of his life; he wasn't sure what he would do without them.

Thinking about the Garins naturally led his thoughts back to Natasha. Every time he thought he had that woman out of his head—and his heart—she somehow wormed her way back in.

Mason had been in love with Natasha Garin, in varying degrees, his entire life. He still remembered the first time he had seen her almost twenty years ago.

He and his mom had just moved into their new house—bought and paid for by his mom's ex-husband. She sent Mason outside to make friends while she unpacked the house. The minute he hit the sidewalk, he heard someone yelling. Since Mason was a naturally curious child and not afraid of the unknown, he'd followed the sound. To his surprise, he found a tiny red-haired girl, sitting on a boy in the middle of the lawn three houses down the street.

"What are you looking at, nerd?" the girl snapped when he stopped in front of them.

Mason crossed his arms over his chest. "What are you doing to him?"

"What does it look like I'm doing?" the little girl said. "I'm sitting on him."

"Why?" Mason asked.

The girl shrugged. "Because he's my brother and I can."

"Get off me, Nattie," the boy yelled.

"Or what, you'll tell Mom again?" She flicked him on the forehead. "Be quiet while I talk to the new kid." She turned back to Mason. "I'm Natasha, and this is my twin brother, Nathaniel."

Mason narrowed his eyes at the word "twin." "You're not twins," he said matter-of-factly.

"Uh, yeah we are, doofus." She poked Nathaniel in the back of the head. "We're the kind of twins that don't look like each other. Anyway, what's *your* name?"

"Mason. I live down there." He pointed toward his new house. "Mom sent me out here to make friends."

Quick as lightning, the boy—Nathaniel—grabbed Natasha by the waist, flipped her over, and shot to his feet. "You live here? Finally, another guy in the neighborhood." He glanced at his sister on the ground. "Now I won't have to hang out with my sister anymore."

Natasha jumped to her feet, tackled Nathaniel around the knees, and forced him to the ground. She was screaming and yelling something Mason couldn't understand, but at that moment his heart twisted in his chest, and Natasha Garin took up residence.

The three of them became best friends. They were always together, especially in elementary school. If the Garin twins were around, you could bet Mason Adler was there, too, and it stayed like that through junior high and their freshman year of high school.

Their sophomore year of high school, Natasha started going her own way and doing her own thing. When Mason and Nate tried to get her to hang out with them, she'd spout some line about three being a crowd and vanish with her friends. While they all remained friends, Natasha purposely separated herself from her brother and Mason, hell-bent on doing her own thing without their interference.

Even when they all went to Lakeside to attend school at the town's private college, she'd refused their offer to share a place to live. Instead, she moved in with Avery, a friend she met at school. Nate chalked it up to Natasha needing to separate herself from her twin and do something on her own; Mason was the collateral damage.

For the last eight years, he had watched Natasha get involved in one relationship after another, each of them ending in heartache for her. First had been Reggie, a football player and gigantic jerk. Not that Natasha had seen that side of him, because she didn't want to see it. After Reggie, she'd started dating some guy named Mike, a college sophomore she met on a trip to Missoula. Natasha couldn't be bothered to give Mason the time of day after Mike came along.

After Mike broke up with her, because she was too young, Natasha dated the captain of the basketball team, Dave. They broke up right before graduation—Mason never knew why—and Natasha retreated into herself, swearing off men. That lasted until the trio left for Lakeside, where she met a guy named Bobby. They dated off and on, and Natasha did her best to distance herself from her brother and Mason.

After every one of the breakups, Mason was there to pick up the pieces. Natasha would be heartbroken, and Mason would be there to take her out for chocolate ice cream with rainbow sprinkles and give her a shoulder to cry on. It was what he did; he was the good guy.

Mason didn't know Natasha was dating Brick until she breezed into Nate's bar one night, her new boyfriend in tow. Mason's dislike for him was instantaneous. Brick seemed nice enough, probably on his best behavior to impress Natasha's twin, but something about him didn't sit right with Mason. Or Nate.

He'd tried to be happy for Natasha when she started dating Brick, he really had, but that had quickly soured when he realized how awful Brick truly was. Mason couldn't understand why Natasha couldn't see it, but his and Nate's dislike of Brick only helped to push Natasha away.

The memories of Natasha's urge to separate herself from the people who cared about her weighed heavily on Mason's heart. Determined to get his mind off his best friend's sister, Mason made his way through the studio to the office in the back. He turned on the computer and opened the week's schedule. Summer was always busy—weddings, reunions, special events in the towns around Flathead Lake, even out-of-state visitors booking family photos while on vacation in order to take advantage of the lake's beauty. It looked like Mason's loaded schedule would go a long way toward getting his mind off Natasha.

On top of Mason's full photography schedule, he also worked part-time as an EMT for the small hospital in town, working two nights a week and on call on the weekends. It kept him busy and out of the house most days. He hadn't realized what a relief that schedule could be until Natasha landed on their doorstep in the middle of the night.

Maybe I'll add a couple nights to my rotation.

Avoiding Natasha might be the only way to maintain his sanity. That woman had him all twisted up inside— she had for years. However, living in the same house with her might push him over the edge, as having her in such close proximity would make it impossible to fight his feelings for her.

Mason shoved himself away from the desk, grabbed his camera, and stepped out of the back door onto a porch that stretched the length of the studio, overlooking Flathead Lake.

Without overthinking it, he snapped a photo of a robin pulling a worm from the dirt under a tree by the lake. Then he took another photo of a gull soaring over the water, looking for fish. The sun and the leaves from the tree created an interesting, dappled green pattern on the water, so Mason quickly took a shot before the sun shifted or the wind blew, changing it.

Three hundred yards down the road, Mason could just make out the back of the Time Out Bar and Grill. That, of course, just made him think of Natasha. Again.

Over the years, guys had come and gone from Natasha's life. Every one of them had left her heartbroken, and Mason had done his best to pick up the pieces, he and Nate.

Maybe this time, Natasha would notice that Mason was always there, waiting in the wings: ready to hold her hand like a good friend, console her with ice cream, and heal her broken heart. Except he was tired of being the friend who helped her get over her heartbreak and move on. He wanted more.

Not that he'd ever get more from her. Natasha would always see him as her brother's best friend, the skinny, gawky kid who lived down the street and monopolized her twin brother's time. She would never see Mason as anything beyond what he'd always been—a friend.

"Mason?"

He took a couple more photos before heading back inside to talk to the person who called him. His boss, Harry, sat at the computer, scrolling through the calendar.

"Hey, Mr. Ward. I thought you were going to Missoula today." Mason closed the door, set his camera down, and sat down across from Harry. "Did you want to take a couple shoots today?"

Harry shook his head. "No, you can do them. I am heading to Missoula, but I wanted to stop and talk to you." Harry sat back in the chair and crossed his arms. "Do you enjoy working here, Mason?"

He nodded. "Yes, sir. I love working here." He cleared his throat. "Why do you ask?"

"You do great work," Harry continued, as if Mason hadn't said anything. "Your photographs are on par with stuff I've seen in upper echelon magazines. Impressive."

"Thank you," Mason murmured.

"You've taken this studio to a whole new level. I can't remember a summer when our calendar was full like this." Harry pointed at the computer. "That's because of you, young man."

Mason shook his head, as heat flooded his cheeks. "No sir, you're exaggerating."

Harry laughed. "No, I'm not. I've still got people sitting in the studio or bunched up in awkward family poses. You don't do that; you have a knack for catching people looking natural, comfortable. They look like they're having fun and enjoying themselves. Those are the photos people want, not the stuff I do."

"Mr. Ward, are you closing up shop and moving to Missoula?" Mason asked.

Harry chuckled and shook his head. "Straight to the point, huh? I always liked that about you. To answer your question, yes, I *am* moving to Missoula. But I'm not closing the studio— I'm selling it. Hopefully, to you."

Mason sat back in stunned silence. It took him a few seconds to wrap his head around what Harry said. "You want to sell the business to me?"

"I'd like to," Harry said. "Give me a couple of days to come up with a number, and I'll present it to you. We'll go from there. And do me a favor; keep this to yourself until everything is completed, okay?"

"Um, yeah, okay." Mason's head spun with the possibilities. "I, uh, guess I can do that."

Harry nodded and pushed himself away from the computer. He clapped Mason on the back as he walked past him. "I'll talk to you later this week, Mason. In the meantime, get to work."

"Yes, sir," Mason replied. He wasn't sure how he could concentrate with all the thoughts spinning around his head. This took his hobby-turned-job to a whole new level. However, he wasn't even sure buying the studio was a possibility; it wasn't like he was rolling in money.

Mason took a deep breath to center himself. Too much had happened in the last twelve hours, so he needed to get out of his own head and get to work. That might be the only thing that would take his mind off his crazy life.

Chapter 3

Natasha

After the boys left for work, Natasha wandered around the small house. She had only been here two or three times since Nate moved in. A pang of regret hit her, as she realized how little time she'd spent with her twin brother during the last few years. Yet he hadn't hesitated to take her in when she needed help.

The house had two bedrooms, one bathroom, a large living room and kitchen, and a small backyard with a decent-sized patio. There was a small foyer by the front door that led directly into the living room.

If she was going to live in such a small house with two single men, they needed to establish some ground rules. Foremost, no one leaves the bathroom without clothes on their body; towels did not count. Her heart nearly stopped when Mason's towel slipped, and she got an eyeful of Mason's manhood. Damn, he grew up well.

Sometimes when she looked at Mason, she still saw the skinny kid who had been best friends with Nate since they were six. The skinny kid who had *always* been at their house, plotted pranks with her twin, and slept on couch cushions on Nate's bedroom floor. The skinny kid who sometimes took her brother away from her when she needed him most. Natasha forgot that the kid grew up to be a hulking 250 lb. giant, with muscles bursting from the seams of his shirt and an ass made for biting.

Natasha closed her eyes and took a deep breath. It was too easy to fantasize about Mason; the man was literally made for it. He could have graced the cover of any bodice-ripping romance novel. His flowing black locks and taut abdomen begged women to fawn over him; it had been like that since their senior year of high school. She still wasn't sure how she'd resisted his charms. The man was a walking romance ad.

But she shouldn't be thinking about Mason like that; she had Brick.

Except she didn't have Brick, not anymore. The realization was a slap to the face. That bitch with her legs in the air, moaning loud enough to rattle the glass in the window, while Natasha's fiancé pounded into her in every way imaginable, she was the one who had Brick. Natasha didn't have anyone.

Natasha dug her phone out of her backpack, called the theater, and told them she was sick. She couldn't face rehearsals and stage manager duties when she was an emotional wreck. After she hung up, she headed for the kitchen. Nate and Mason didn't have much to eat: a bunch of kids cereals, chips, dip, a couple of soup cans with dust on them, leftover pizza, and beer—lots and lots of beer.

"Doesn't Nate get enough to drink at the bar?" she muttered. Her brother owned and operated the Time Out Bar and Grill, one of the most popular bars in Lakeside, especially with the college students who attended Lakeside College.

Natasha grabbed a box of Lucky Charms, returned to the couch, found a Disney movie on one of the streaming channels, and buried herself under the covers on the couch. She would stay there until her brother got home, and maybe then she'd deal with the shambles her life had become. Until then, she intended to pretend everything was copacetic.

Except she couldn't stop replaying every minute of the last two years, wondering why she had been so blind to how truly awful Brick was to her.

Jason "Brick" Brickman came into her life her sophomore year of college. He wasn't the type of guy she normally dated—he was edgy, dangerous, a bad boy. The exact opposite of tooth-rotting nice guy, Mason Adler. She refused to acknowledge that her relationship with Brick began at the same time Mason started dating a pretty blonde waitress from the Time Out Bar and Grill. The two had *nothing* to do with each other.

Brick swept her off her feet. Everyone told her he was a jerk, a fact obvious to everyone who knew him. They tried to get Natasha to see it and she did, but she also swore there was a sweet side to Brick, something he kept hidden from others. Natasha dealt with him being an asshole because she believed he loved her, or maybe she *hoped* he loved her.

After they got engaged and moved in together, that sweet side of Brick seemed to disappear. Desperate to keep her relationship together, and unable to admit she made a mistake—again—Natasha turned a blind eye to Brick's lies, his late nights out, his constant drinking, and his inability to keep a job for longer than a few months. Even his refusal to set a wedding date almost a year into their engagement didn't deter her from staying with him. It was easier to ignore Brick's bullshit than it was to break up with him. Their entwined, tangled lives made it impossible to be apart; being with Brick was easier than being alone.

"God, I'm an idiot," she said out loud. Laying it all out in her head had Natasha wondering if she'd lost her mind. She couldn't believe she allowed Brick to treat her so shoddily. She deserved better. Hell, she wanted better.

The realization brought the tears with it. It wasn't long before she had the blanket pressed against her face, sobbing into it. The weight of everything that happened sat heavy on her chest, making it hard to breathe. Natasha couldn't keep giving all of herself to someone who gave her nothing in return.

Her sobs tapered off, and she closed her eyes in exhaustion. She must have fallen asleep because the next thing she knew, the front door slammed closed, and Nate's and Mason's voices echoed through the small house. She groaned and struggled to sit up. She'd been asleep for hours.

Nate stalked across the room, grabbed her ankle, and tugged her down the length of the couch until her ass hung off the edge. She kicked him with her free foot, barely missing his crotch and earning a laugh from Mason.

"Wake up, sunshine," Nate said. "We got Roselli's." He frowned at the half-eaten box of Lucky Charms˙ on the coffee table. "You need some proper food. After we eat, we're going to get your stuff. I grabbed some empty boxes from the bar."

Natasha shook her head. "I don't want to go pick up my things. What if Brick is there? I don't know if I can handle seeing him right now."

Nate rolled his eyes. "If he's there, he's there. You'll tell him it's over. For good this time. It's time to put that jerk in his place. Confront him once and for all. You need the closure, sooner rather than later. The longer you wait, the more likely it is the asshole will think you'll take him back." He yanked on her leg again. "Don't argue with me; you know I'm right. Now, come eat so we can get going."

Natasha glared at her brother and prayed he would burst into flames. When he didn't, she sighed heavily, pushed herself off the couch, and followed Nate into the kitchen. Two boxes of Roselli's pizza sat in the middle of the table. Mason pulled paper plates from the cupboard and dropped them on the table. She slid into an empty chair.

Mason set a bottle of water in front of her. "Looks like you need this."

"Thanks." She could always count on him to look out for her.

The three of them ate in silence, her and Nate staring at each other across the table. Poor Mason—no stranger to their standoffs—tried to look anywhere but at the stewing brother and sister. After five minutes of uncomfortable silence, Natasha sat forward, her elbows on the table.

"Nate, listen to me—."

"I have listened to you," Nate interjected. "I have listened to you bitch about Brick for more than a year. I have dried your tears; I have turned the other cheek when that asshole has treated you like shit. I have held my tongue for too long. Not anymore. We're going over there, and you are telling him that the two of you are finished. Period."

Natasha took a deep breath and swallowed past the lump rising in her throat. She didn't want to cry. Again. "Nate, seriously, for once in your life, listen to the words coming out of my mouth. Please try to understand what I'm going through right now. I'm not ... I can't see Brick. I just can't. Not yet, not with the image of him and that girl still fresh in my mind. Please, I'm begging you to understand."

She could feel the tickle at the back of her throat, and the tears pricking at her eyes. So much for not crying; the tears slid down her face. She plucked a napkin from the stack next to the pizza box and wiped her face. Her hands shook, and she couldn't talk above a whisper, fearful she would start sobbing again.

"I know what I need to do. I do," she continued. "Ending it with Brick is my only option. And I will, I swear. But I cannot do it tonight. I just can't. I need time to process everything. This is ... this decision changes my whole life."

"You need a clean break, Tash," Nate argued. "You need to go over there and tell him to fuck off. You'll feel better once you do."

Natasha nodded. *God, that would feel good.* But just thinking about it made her stomach twist into uncomfortable knots. She took a deep breath to calm herself before she spoke. "I know, Nate. I know you're right. But ... but I'm not like you; I can't turn off my emotions just like that." Natasha snapped her fingers.

"We're not talking about me, Tash. We're talking about you."

Natasha pinched the bridge of her nose. "Yes, we're talking about me, which is why you need to listen to what I'm saying. I am done with Brick. I swear. He and I are over. And I will tell him when I'm ready. Just don't make me see him today; it has been less than twenty-four hours since I found him naked in our bed with another woman. I cannot face him today. I can't listen to his excuses and his patronizing tone."

Nate opened his mouth, but before he could say anything, Mason interrupted them.

"Give her a break, Nate," he said. His eyes flashed with an emotion Natasha was afraid to analyze. "I know you want to watch her tear Brick a new one, but she's hurting. Let her stay here while we go get her things. She can destroy him later, and you can watch. Right, Tasha?"

Natasha nodded. "Yes. Th-that ... that sounds—" Her voice cracked, and she swallowed thickly. She stared at the top of the table, the napkin pressed to her lips.

"Okay," Nate said. He reached across the table and squeezed her hand. "It's okay, sis. I'm sorry. I guess I didn't realize how you felt. Mace and I will go get all your stuff. Don't worry about it."

Natasha couldn't speak, so she nodded. She took a sip of her water as relief washed over her. When she caught Mason's eye a few minutes later, she mouthed "Thank you," to him. He nodded and shrugged one shoulder, a faint smile on his face.

Mason was a good guy.

Chapter 4

Mason

"Nate, you need to give Tasha a break," Mason said. "This can't be easy for her."

"Brick is an ass," Nate muttered. "She needs to tell him off, once and for all. You know I'm right."

Mason sighed. "I know, but it needs to be on her own terms. Not because her brother tells her to do it."

"You know, if you had just told her three or four years ago how you feel about her—"

"*Felt*," Mason interrupted. "How I *felt* about her. Past tense." He pulled into one of the parking spots in front of Natasha's place and put the truck in gear, shoving open the door and stepping out. Mason could feel Nate's eyes boring a hole into the back of his head as he left the truck.

Nate climbed out and shot his best friend a dirty look. "Uh huh, sure. Don't lie to me. You know damn well it isn't past tense." He shook his head. "I'm just saying, if you told Tasha how you felt in high school, or middle school, or elementary school, or at some point in our lives, we wouldn't be standing in front of her apartment, ready to move her shit out. She wouldn't be forced to live with us, and she wouldn't be crying herself to sleep at night on our couch. Instead, she'd be gladly living with us, sleeping in *your* bed, and a million times happier than she is now."

"Shut up," Mason grumbled.

Nate shook his head. "I think I'm done shutting up about this." He must have seen the terrified look on Mason's face because he chuckled. "Oh, don't worry, I won't out you to my sister. But I think it's time the two of you stopped this weird dance you've been doing for the last twenty years and figure out what you want. The two of you should be together. Problem is, neither of you knows it."

"Okay, you're right. I know how I feel about Tasha. I've always known how I feel about her." Mason snorted. "I have it more than figured out. I've tried to fight my feelings for her, and I can't. But I will not tell her when she is vulnerable and hurt."

"I think she deserves to know," Nate said. "So why won't you tell her?"

Mason pinched the bridge of his nose. "Because right now, knowing Tasha, she would feel obligated to let me down easy, which would just make everything worse. It can wait."

"If you wait too long, you'll lose her again," Nate said.

Nate was right; this was a familiar dance in their lives. Mason waited too long to make his move, and Natasha moved on to someone else.

Mason didn't want to talk about it, so he grunted, crossed his arms over his chest, and nodded at the door.

"I don't want to discuss this anymore. Can we please get this over with?"

Nate dug Natasha's keys out of his pocket and headed upstairs. Mason followed him and leaned against the wall, while Nate pounded on the apartment door.

When no one answered, Nate waited thirty seconds and knocked again. Only then did he use Natasha's keys to unlock the door. The apartment was eerily quiet and obviously empty. Following the directions Natasha texted him, Nate ordered Mason to gather her stuff from the living room while he headed for the bedroom, with a box tucked under his arm.

Mason did as Nate asked. Before he looked for Natasha's things, he stood in the middle of the living room and took everything in. The apartment was dark and dreary, thanks to the drawn blinds. The stench of Brick's cigarette smoke, beer, and stale sweat permeated the air. Empty beer bottles laid on the floor and coffee table next to an over-flowing ashtray, and an immense pile of dirty clothes dominated the floor next to a beat-up recliner. Mason couldn't imagine Natasha in this depressing place. She was such a bright person, bubbling with life. It hurt Mason's heart to think that Brick had slowly stolen that light from her, changing the girl Mason loved into a shadowy version of herself. Thank God she was getting away from him.

"Mason!"

"Yeah! Coming!" He followed the sound of Nate's voice to the back of the apartment.

Forty-five minutes later, Mason leaned against the truck while Nate made one more sweep of the apartment. They grabbed everything they could, calling Natasha several times to make sure they looked in all the right places.

Nate was on his way out the door of the complex when a loud, drunk voice shouted from up the street.

"What the fuck you doin' here?" The words were slurred so badly, they were practically indecipherable.

Brick staggered up the street with a plastic bag filled with liquor bottles dangling from his fingers, his hair stuck up all over his head, and his t-shirt on backwards. He stopped a few feet from the truck and eyed the boxes stacked in the back. "What the hell are you doing? What's in those boxes?" He glared at them with red-rimmed eyes.

"What does it look like we're doing?" Mason asked.

Brick snarled. "It looks like you're robbing me blind."

Nate stalked the short distance from the apartment entrance to where Brick stood on the sidewalk. "We aren't robbing you, asshole. We're picking up my sister's things. She's done with you."

Brick snorted. "She'll be back. Nat always comes back to me. As soon as she stops pouting and answers her damn phone, I'll convince her to come back. She'll forgive me. She always does. So, you might as well put her stuff back."

Nate shook his head and clenched his fists. "Not this time. She won't come back."

Brick laughed, an ugly, thick, wicked laugh that made Mason's skin crawl. "Trust me, Nate, she'll be back. Nobody else will fuck her, so it's just a matter of time before she comes back to the only man who will."

Nate's face contorted into a mask of pure hatred, and he launched himself at Brick, connecting his fist with Brick's chin to make a resounding crack. Brick stumbled back and fell on his ass. Nate took a step toward him, but Mason lunged after him and grabbed his friend before Nate could jump on Brick and beat him into oblivion.

"Get in the truck, Nate. He's not worth it," Mason said.

"Did you hear what he said about my sister?" Nate bellowed, struggling to get away from Mason. "I'm going to fucking kill him."

"I heard what he said," Mason interjected. "Believe me, I heard it." He wanted to rip Brick's tongue out and make him eat it, but that wouldn't solve anything. Instead, he shoved Nate into the truck. "Stay put." He slammed the door harder than he intended, but he barely held his anger in check. Nate was right. Brick deserved a fist to the face, maybe more, but it wasn't their place to dole out his punishment; that was up to Natasha.

When Mason turned around, Brick had pushed himself to his feet. He wiped his hand across his lips and stared at the blood on his fingers. He wobbled unsteadily as he pointed at the truck. "Get out of my way, Adler." He took a step toward Mason, headed toward the truck and Nate.

Mason shook his head. "Let it go, Brick. You're lucky I didn't let him kill you. You certainly deserve it."

"Fuck you," Brick snapped. "You love this. You've been mooning over Nat for years. Don't get too excited, though. She wants a real man. Like I said, she'll come crawling back to me."

"Stay away from Tasha," Mason ordered. "Or you'll regret it."

Mason marched around the truck, yanked open the door, and climbed inside. Brick screamed and cursed at him every step of the way. Mason swore he could still hear him, even as the truck rounded the corner.

—

Natasha stood at the door when they came back. "Well, how'd it go?" she asked.

"Your brother punched Brick, knocked him to the ground," Mason said.

Natasha put her hands on her hips and stared at the ceiling. "Please tell me you didn't?"

Nate grinned. "Oh, I did. The bastard deserved it, too. I would have done worse if Mace hadn't pulled me off him and forced me to leave."

Mason snorted. "I don't have the cash to bail you out of jail. Save it for another day."

"Did he ... did Brick say anything?" Natasha interjected. "Did he seem sorry?"

Nate shook his head. "Honestly, he didn't seem to give a shit." He gave her a one-armed hug and kissed her temple. "He also said some really crappy things about you, Tash. That's why I decked him. He's lucky I didn't kill him."

A grimace marred Natasha's pretty face and her shoulders slumped. Before she dropped her head to stare at the floor, Mason saw tears glistening in her eyes. She extricated herself from her brother's grip, slipped her shoes on, pushed past Mason, and headed for his truck.

"I'm grabbing a beer before we unload," Nate said. "Do you want one?"

"Yeah, grab me one. I'm gonna go help Tasha bring her stuff in." He set the grocery bag in his hand on the table and headed outside.

Natasha had the tailgate down, yanking boxes off the truck while muttering under her breath the entire time. She stopped to open a couple of them and peer inside, which only seemed to make her more irritated. She grabbed the heaviest box and before Mason could rush to help her, it slipped from her hands and fell to the ground, spilling its contents across the driveway. Natasha kicked a shoe before leaning against the side of the truck with her head in her hands.

Mason walked down the sidewalk and stood beside her. He put a hand on the small of her back and rested his chin on top of her head. "Hey, it's okay," he whispered.

"It's not, though," she muttered, her voice catching on the last word. "Brick played me for a fool. I gave him everything and in return, I got shit. I was so stupid."

"You weren't stupid," Mason said. "You were in love."

Natasha scoffed. "No, I don't think I was. Maybe at first I thought I was in love, but I think over the last few months, I realized Brick wasn't the guy I'm supposed to be with. I chose him when I was really vulnerable and looking for somebody, anybody, to fill the hole in my heart. Brick was there; I thought he was the one. I was wrong."

Mason closed his eyes and hugged Natasha closer. "Who do you think you're meant to be with, if it's not Brick?" Deep down, he knew it wasn't him, but that didn't stop him from wishing it was.

Natasha stiffened in his arms and pulled away. "I ... I don't know. Maybe I'll never know." She grabbed a box off the ground and tucked it under her arm. "Let's get my stuff inside. We can shove it in the corner of Nate's room."

"I don't think so," Nate yelled from the front porch. He held up two bottles of beer. "Who wants a beer? I know I do!"

Natasha laughed and shook her head. "I hate beer. You know what I need?"

"Chocolate ice cream and rainbow sprinkles?" Mason replied.

She turned to look at Mason, a faint smile on her lips. "Yeah, that's exactly what I need."

"Good, because I stopped at the store and grabbed some. It's on the table."

Natasha smiled at him, and it broke his heart. "You're such a great guy, Mace. I knew I could count on you. Let's go drown my sorrows in ice cream."

Mason nodded and followed her inside. She'd piqued his curiosity; who did Natasha think she was meant to be with? Would she tell him? He certainly planned on getting some answers out of her.

Chapter 5

Natasha

Natasha sat in the large, overstuffed chair in the corner of the living room. She kept a wary eye on the slightly chaotic group of people surrounding her. Nate, Mason, and their friends Oscar and Gavin were in front of the big screen TV—a TV that was too big for their small house, in her opinion. Yelling and cursing filled the room as they watched a baseball game. She didn't know who was playing, or who was winning or losing, but she really didn't care. The noise and chaos helped keep her mind off the sorry state of her life.

She had lived with her brother and Mason for three weeks at that point. Three endless weeks. It wasn't like she wasn't grateful that her brother had given her a place to stay, because she was. But some days, she felt like they were back in junior high. Nate enjoyed teasing her and harassing her—as any older brother liked to do—and

Mason tiptoed around her like he was afraid she would break down at any minute.

Natasha had to admit she had been emotional, off and on, during the last three weeks, but she was finally getting the tears and the "woe is me" attitude under control. It helped to remember how she had found Brick in bed with another woman, how he'd avoided setting an actual wedding date, and how he treated her like his maid and cook rather than his girlfriend or fiancée.

Sometimes things with Nate and especially Mason were awkward, but mostly it was good. Occasionally she caught one of them walking around in their underwear, though they'd gotten better at wearing pants around the apartment, even if they had a hard time finding a shirt. There had been no more glimpses of wet, naked bodies after a shower. She had to admit, with Mason, there may have been some regret that he kept himself covered up. Nate kept drinking her orange juice, stealing her frozen lunches, and eating her granola bars. Mason liked to drink her Coke Zeroes, and he'd eaten an entire box of cookies she'd bought. She couldn't stay mad at him, though; he'd replaced both of them for her.

Since moving in with her brother, she had learned—to her perpetual irritation—her brother was quite the ladies' man. There were phone calls, constant dates, and women she didn't know sneaking in and out of his bedroom at all hours of the night, women she inevitably got to see since her bed was the couch in the living room. Nate had been with so many women, she couldn't keep track of them all. When she asked him about it, he smiled, shrugged, kissed her cheek, and walked away happily whistling.

Mason didn't seem to have a girlfriend at the moment. He'd broken up with the pretty blonde waitress, Allison, more than a year ago and, as far as Natasha knew, he hadn't dated anyone since. This secretly pleased her, which didn't make sense, given her current dating situation, but she didn't want him to have a girlfriend. A hard knot of jealously formed in the pit of her stomach at the thought. She hated to call it jealousy, but she had to be honest with herself. She realized for years she had been jealous of any woman who got Mason's attention.

Her phone vibrated against her leg. Before she picked it up, she took another drink from the glass of wine in her hand. In the last ten minutes, five text messages had come from Brick. It brought the total for the day to roughly twenty, give or take a few. So far, she'd resisted the urge to answer him.

Vera, another friend of the boys, was perched on the arm of the chair. "Hey Tasha, how are things going? Are you settling in?"

Natasha shrugged. "I guess so. As much as one can when the couch in the living room is your bed, and you're living with two single men who sometimes still act like they're in junior high."

Vera laughed. "They're bachelors. They haven't had to answer to anyone but each other for a long time. There are no rules in this house."

Natasha snorted. "There are now. Rule number one is everybody wears pants." The sight of a very naked, well-endowed Mason flashed through her head.

Vera laughed. "Well, there you go. You're making rules, fitting right in. Are the boys adhering to rule number one?"

"Sometimes," Natasha replied. "They still don't clean up after themselves. The TV is always on something related to sports, and the only food in this house comes from a package or a restaurant."

"You'll get used to it," Vera said. "Besides, you won't be here for long, right? Nate said your stay here was temporary?"

"Hopefully, I'll just be here until I can get back on my feet. Only two or three months at the most."

"See? You only have to put up with it for a couple of months. Easy peasy." Vera patted her on the shoulder before she got up and marched into the middle of the chaotic men watching the game. She whispered something in Oscar's ear that earned her a smile. Oscar laughed and pointed at the TV, obviously explaining the game to her. It was obvious they were interested in each other.

Natasha's phone vibrated against her leg. Again. She peeked at it. Text number six. She didn't have time to read it though because Summer, Gavin's girlfriend and another friend from high school, squeezed into the chair beside her.

"They're a little overwhelming, aren't they?"

Natasha nodded. She'd been fielding questions and comments like this all night from everyone. Natasha suspected one or both of the boys had told everyone to play nice with Nate's depressed sister. Even Oscar and Gavin had stopped to console her because of her current living arrangements. She didn't know if it irritated her or pleased her.

Summer dug her elbow into Natasha's side. "Earth to Nat."

"Sorry," she mumbled. "I zoned out."

Her brain had been like Swiss cheese since the breakup. She couldn't remember if she was coming or going, alive or dead, happy or sad. The only thing she knew for sure was that she couldn't seem to move on, to get out of the funk she was in. She couldn't get over Brick.

As if on cue, the phone tucked under her leg vibrated. She closed her eyes and exhaled. Maybe she couldn't get over him because he wouldn't leave her alone. The constant barrage of texts and voicemails was getting to her, wearing her down.

Summer poked her in the side. "What's going on? You've been moping in the corner all night, staring at your phone and sucking on your wine."

Natasha shrugged. "It's Brick. He's bombarding me with texts and voicemails. He won't leave me alone."

Summer rubbed her leg. "I'm sorry, sweetie." She rested her head against Natasha's. "What are you going to do?"

"Sick my brother on him?" Natasha giggled.

Summer snorted. "Nate would gladly kick Brick's ass."

"He already did," Natasha muttered.

"What?" Summer squeezed her hand so hard it hurt. "You're kidding?"

"When they went to pick up my stuff, I guess Brick showed up, and they got into it."

"Shut up!" Summer laughed. "That sounds like Nathaniel. He is always coming to your rescue, he and Mason both." She looked at Tasha out of the corner of her eye. "Hey, did you know Mason is single?"

Natasha rolled her eyes. "Of course, I do. What does that have to do with anything?"

"Well, you're single, *he's* single." Summer grinned and wiggled her eyebrows. "Maybe there's something there?"

Natasha couldn't help it; she laughed. "I don't think so. Mason is my friend. That's it." Her phone vibrated, more than once. She pulled it out from under her leg. This time, Brick was calling. She hit the button on the side twice and stuck it back under her leg.

"Summer!" Gavin yelled from the other side of the room.

"Give me a minute!" Summer turned back to Natasha. "Don't let Brick get to you. Ignore him, block his number, anything to get him off your case. You deserve better, sweetie. Maybe that something better is Mason."

"You're being ridiculous." Natasha downed the rest of her glass of wine, got to her feet, and went into the kitchen. She grabbed the bottle from the counter and refilled her glass. She needed to get drunk and dull her senses so she didn't feel anything. Summer followed her, then stood right beside her, staring at her.

"You're both single, and you're both lonely," she said.

"How do you know Mason is lonely?" Natasha asked. "Did he tell you he was lonely?"

"I've known Mason for almost as long as you and yes, I can tell he's lonely." Summer stepped closer to Natasha and lowered her voice. "He's always the third or the fifth wheel, the guy who sits in the corner while the couples have fun. He's always got that mopey smile on his face, the one that screams 'I'm not happy, but I'm gonna fake it until I make it.' You know which one I'm talking about." She reached out and squeezed Natasha's arm. "It's the same smile you've had on your face for the last few weeks."

Natasha grimaced. "Gee, thanks Summer. I'm so glad you've got me all figured out." She crossed her arms over her chest, her wine glass dangling between two fingers. "You know that I just broke up with Brick three weeks ago.

I am not ready for another relationship. Not right now. I need time to mourn the one I lost."

"Brick's an asshole," Summer said. "He always has been. I think you figured that out a while ago. You're just afraid to admit it's been over between the two of you for a long time. He's out of your life for good. You need to move on. Why don't you go after the good guy for a change?"

"Mason and I are friends; that's it. If there was ever a time for us, I'm pretty sure it's passed. I am nothing more than his best friend's sister. I'm not sure I've ever been anything more to him than Nate's twin sister. After everything I've gone through, I need time to get my life in order. I'm not in the mood to put myself out there to get rejected."

"You don't know that he'll reject you," Summer argued.

"He will. Trust me. Like I said, we're friends, nothing more. Besides, it would be pretty shitty of me to pursue someone a few weeks after dumping my fiancé. Besides, if Mason had feelings for me, he would have said something."

"Maybe he never got the chance," Summer pointed out. She pushed a hand through her hair and sighed. "There always seems to be someone in the way."

Natasha glanced into the living room, but everyone was engrossed in the game. She lowered her voice anyway. "I don't have feelings for Mason. If I ever did, it was some dumb fleeting moment back in junior high. There is nothing between us."

"Bullshit," Summer muttered. "You went out and found a guy who was the polar opposite of Mason because you had feelings for Mason, and it hurt you when he dated Allison. Finding someone who was so completely different from Mace was your way of saying 'F you' to the guy you really cared about."

Natasha rubbed a hand over the back of her neck and grimaced. This conversation irritated her. "I don't want to have this discussion anymore. Can we change the subject, please? I ... I just can't talk about this anymore."

Summer rubbed Natasha's arm. "I'm sorry, Tash. I'll back off."

"Thank you." Natasha rubbed her forehead; she could feel a headache coming on.

Gavin let out a loud whoop, drawing Summer's attention away from Natasha. She squeezed Natasha's hand, skipped out of the kitchen, and leaped into her boyfriend's arms, giggling as he kissed her neck.

The phone in Natasha's back pocket vibrated again. She yanked it out and looked at it. It was Brick. Again. She had just enough time to shove it in her back pocket before Nate appeared at her side, grabbed her hand, and dragged her into the living room.

"Come on, sis. Remember when we used to watch the Mariners as kids? Come watch with us. It'll be fun, just like old times."

Natasha took a huge swallow of her wine and glanced at Mason out of the corner of her eye. "Sure, fun. Just like when we were kids."

Chapter 6

Mason

*O*nce the Mariners lost, the party was over. Oscar and Vera left to get something to eat, followed by Summer and Gavin. After a call from Brooke, Nate's assistant manager at the bar, Nate left to deal with a bar-related emergency, leaving Mason home alone with Natasha. He had no idea where she was; like everyone else, she had disappeared after the party broke up.

It didn't surprise Mason that everyone had disappeared, leaving him to clean up the mess. He was always on clean-up duty, especially since he was the odd man out. Everyone else had a significant other or was working on getting a significant other, except for him. It left him to clean up messes, pay bar tabs, and act as the designated driver. Mason didn't argue; he was happy to help his friends, though it got a little old after a while.

He tossed the beer bottles in the recycle can, stacked the empty pizza boxes on the table, and turned off all the lights, except the one over the stove and the light in the small foyer. He checked his watch before he flopped down on the couch and closed his eyes. It was after eleven, and he was exhausted. He needed to go to bed and get some sleep; he had a photography appointment early in the morning.

Mason knew he would need to move soon so Natasha could have her bed, but he was tired. He'd move when she told him to move. Besides, it gave him an excuse to spend time with her when she reappeared.

After a few minutes, he heard the faint sound of her voice, getting louder by the second. He pushed himself to his feet with a grunt and followed the sound to the small patio at the back of the house. The door was open a crack, and he could hear Natasha on her phone.

"I can't, Brick," she said. "I don't think you understand what you did to me. I will never get the image of you with that woman out of my head."

Mason moved the curtain covering the sliding glass door aside with one finger. Natasha sat on one of the rickety patio chairs, her phone pressed to her ear. He let go of the curtain and leaned against the wall, watching Natasha through the gap in the curtain. He hated to eavesdrop, but he couldn't help himself, not when it came to Natasha. Both he and Nate thought she wasn't talking to Brick; apparently, they were wrong.

"Brick, listen—." Natasha's mouth snapped shut, her lips pursed in a tight line. She squeezed her eyes closed, the porch light illuminating the tears sliding down her cheeks. Her entire body shook as she pressed the phone tight against her face. Mason couldn't tell if she was angry or hurt.

Maybe it's both.

"Goddamn it, Brick; shut up and listen to me!" Natasha yelled. Her voice echoed through the dark night and carried into the house. Even if Mason hadn't been eavesdropping, he would have heard that.

"You're always drunk. You're always sorry. And you always, *always* say it won't happen again. But then, you do it again. And again. How long have I put up with this shit?"

She didn't speak for a few seconds, but her head shook from side to side as she listened to whatever Brick was saying on the other end of the phone.

"I don't deserve this," Natasha whispered. She cleared her throat and spoke louder. "I've been putting up with your shit for too long. I should have realized sooner that I don't deserve to be treated like I don't matter. I never deserved it. I need to be with someone who loves me, cares about me, and puts me first."

A sob tore out of her, the sound so heart-wrenching Mason felt the ache deep in his bones. The need to protect her, to shelter her from any more pain, overwhelmed him.

I'm going to kill Brick if I see him again.

"Don't do that," Natasha continued. "Do *not* throw that in my face again." Another sob escaped her, and she drew in a shaky breath. "He has nothing to do with this. With us. You will not drag him into this and try to deflect the blame off yourself. This is about *you* and the choices you've made in our relationship. I've been more than understanding, and I've tried to be patient. I've given more time and energy to this relationship than I should have. I can't do it anymore. I'm done. It's over. I'll return the engagement ring—."

Brick must have interrupted her because she abruptly stopped talking and rolled her eyes. She listened for a second before she spoke.

"I don't care what you do with it. Pawn it, sell it, give it to the bitch you were fucking. I do not care. I'm returning the ring, and then I do not want to see you again. Ever."

Natasha stabbed at her phone screen, screaming in frustration when it apparently wouldn't do what she wanted.

Mason shoved the door open, stepped outside, and snatched the phone from her hand. On the other end, he heard Brick curse. He ignored it, hit the end button, and shoved the phone in his front pocket. He reached for Natasha, and she didn't hesitate to fall into his arms, her face pressed against his chest as heartbreaking sobs ripped through her. They fell to the couch after he led her inside and across the living room.

Natasha wrapped her arms around Mason, pressed her body tight against his, tucked her head under his chin, and let go. Her tears soaked the front of his shirt, but he didn't care. He held her, rubbed circles on her back, and murmured platitudes meant to comfort, anything to soothe her pain.

She clung to him like a drowning woman holding on to her rescuer. More than anything, Mason wanted to be her rescuer; he wanted to save her from everything and everyone who might hurt her. For now, he would be her friend and hold her until she got it all out.

Once the tears tapered off and the sobs became nothing more than the occasional heaving breath, Natasha twisted her head to look up at him. She gave him a weak smile.

"Thank you, Mason. You're a great friend."

"You're welcome," he whispered.

She took his hand and held it tight. "I don't know what I'd do without you. I love you, Mace."

Mason hugged her tight. "Love you, too." He kissed the top of her head and closed his eyes.

If only you knew how much.

———

"Oh my gosh," a loud voice squealed. "Aren't they just the cutest couple ever?"

"Shh," Nate hissed. "You're going to wake them up. And they aren't a couple, though they should be."

Mason opened his eyes, squinting to see in the dimly lit room. Nate stood behind the couch, smirking at him and Natasha tangled in each other's arms. Some girl Mason had never seen before stood beside Nate, also staring at them. Mason gave Nate a dirty look, waved his fingers, and mouthed, "Go away."

He glanced at Natasha. She was asleep, her red hair falling over her face and her fingers twisted in the hem of his shirt. It was the first time she'd looked content since she moved in with them.

"Comfy?" Nate whispered.

Mason glared at him and put a finger to his lips. Nate nodded, put his hands on the girl's waist, and pushed her toward his bedroom door. A high-pitched giggle burst out of her, the sound like nails on a chalkboard to Mason's ears.

"C'mon, Dottie, let's leave the happy couple alone," Nate whispered. He opened his bedroom door and ushered her inside.

Natasha stirred in Mason's arms. She stretched, her hand smacking him in the face. Her head popped up, and she squinted at him.

"Sorry." She looked around the dark living room. "What time is it?"

"It's okay," he replied. He pushed her hair away from her face before looking at his watch. "It's a little after two."

She nodded. "Wow. I was dead to the world; I haven't slept like that in weeks. Maybe I should sleep with you all the time." She giggled, put her hands on Mason's chest, pushed herself upright, and leaned against him. She bent over and kissed the corner of his mouth.

"Thanks again. Talking to Brick was rough. I appreciate you being there for me when I needed a friend." She kissed the corner of his mouth again before she climbed off him and disappeared into the bathroom.

Mason groaned, rolled to his side, and hugged the pillow to his chest. He willed the feelings and the inappropriate situation stirring in his pants to go away.

What the hell am I doing? What is Tasha doing?

This was too reminiscent of high school and their first two years of college. He'd consoled her after every breakup, the friend perpetually there for her. Then he'd wait around for Natasha to realize he was more than her twin brother's best friend, not just that skinny kid she'd known since first grade. He was someone who could love her like she'd never been loved before.

Mason's phone vibrated in his front pocket, making him jump. He sat up and yanked it free, immediately realizing the rose gold phone in his hand was not his, but Natasha's. He forgot he took it from her earlier and shoved it in his pocket. The screen showed a text message from Brick.

Mason shot a quick look at the closed bathroom door. Guilt tore through him, but it quickly dissipated. He was protecting Natasha; that was all. He took a chance and typed in a passcode—her birthday. The phone opened, so he checked the text message.

[I'm sorry, baby. Let's talk. Call me, please. I will do whatever I have to so you're happy. You name it, and I will do it. I want you back. I love you.]

Anger rushed through him. He wanted nothing more than to tear Brick apart piece by piece, slowly and painfully.

Why won't he let her go? Let her move on?

Another text popped up on the screen.

[I swear I won't mention Mason or his feelings for you again. I'm begging you to give me a chance.]

Confusion replaced the anger. How the hell did Brick know he had feelings for Natasha? It wasn't the first time he'd mentioned it. The only person Mason had ever told was Nate, and both of them had been holding onto that secret for going on twenty years.

Am I that obvious?

Maybe he wasn't as good at hiding his feelings for Natasha as he thought. It had been obvious to Allison, his former girlfriend, and Brick seemed aware of it as well. So much for keeping secrets.

His finger hovered over the messages from Brick. Natasha didn't need to see them. She needed space and time to heal. She needed to move on.

Natasha needed Mason.

The bathroom door opened, and Natasha stepped out, face freshly scrubbed and glowing. For once, she had a smile on her face, one that actually reached her eyes for the first time since her breakup with Brick. She opened the linen closet and started pulling out the sheets and blankets she used for the couch. She glanced at Mason out of the corner of her eye.

"Are you gonna get off my bed or what?" The blanket fell to the floor, so Natasha bent over to pick it up.

While she was preoccupied, Mason swiped left on the messages, hit delete, then he locked the phone. He held it out to Natasha with a forced smile on his face, pushing his anger, confusion, and guilt deep down inside himself.

"Yeah, sorry. Here's your phone." He pressed a chaste kiss to the top of her head. "I'll see you in the morning." He squeezed her shoulder and headed for his room, his heart thumping hard against his ribcage.

Chapter 7

Natasha

I shouldn't have come alone.

Natasha shifted uneasily and knocked on the apartment door again. She checked her watch; it was twenty minutes after four. Brick agreed to meet her there at four, after she left the theater for the day. Not that it surprised her, but he probably forgot.

Just as she turned to leave, the door flew open. Brick stood in front of her, hair a mess, sleep creases on his face, and wearing nothing but a pair of ratty sweatpants. He scrubbed a hand over his face. The smell of alcohol washed over Natasha every time he moved.

"I was asleep." His tone was accusatory, like they hadn't planned to meet, and she had shown up unannounced.

Natasha sighed and clenched her fists. "You knew I was coming. We talked about it."

Brick didn't bother to respond. He opened the door all the way, turned around, and stumbled back into the apartment. Natasha followed him.

She wrinkled her nose and attempted to breathe through her mouth. The sink overflowed with filthy dishes, piles of dirty clothes littered the room, empty liquor bottles laid all over the tables, and ashtrays overflowed in several spots around the room.

Brick grabbed a stained t-shirt from a pile on the couch, held it to his nose, and inhaled deeply before he pulled it on. Then he dropped into his beat-up recliner and stared at her. Natasha opened her purse and took out the box containing the small diamond ring he had given her almost a year ago. She shoved aside one of the overflowing ashtrays and set the box on the table beside his chair.

"As promised, here's the ring." She gripped her purse tight with one hand and took a step backward, moving toward the door.

"So, that's it then?" Brick snapped. "You drop it off and leave? The last two years didn't mean anything to you? You can walk away from our relationship so easily?"

Natasha froze; she'd been afraid of this. Nothing with Brick was easy, and ending their relationship was no exception. She shook her head and met his eyes. "If you can fuck someone else without a second thought, then I can walk away without a glance back."

"Quit throwing that in my goddamn face. I made a mistake. If you'd let me explain—."

Natasha laughed, though this certainly wasn't funny. "Let you explain? Explain what, precisely? I caught you having sex with another woman in our bed; that is not a mistake. You didn't *accidentally* end up with your dick inside of her while she screamed her head off." She took a deep breath and fought the tears threatening to fall. "There is nothing for you to explain. I saw it with my own eyes. Shit, Brick, every time I close my eyes, I see it."

Brick sat forward in his chair and clasped his hands between his legs. He stared up at her, attempting to look endearing. She'd seen it before. "I love you, Nat. Please give me a chance to make it up to you. I'll do anything you want. Please, I am begging you to give me another chance."

Natasha shook her head. Dealing with Brick gave her whiplash. One minute he was an asshole, the next he tried to charm her into taking him back. But this time it wouldn't work.

"No, Brick. I can't. I'm done. I can't be with someone who has no respect for me."

Brick shot to his feet and before she could back away from him, he grabbed her upper arm. "Please, baby." His grip on her tightened. "Let's talk it out. I know we can figure it out if we try. After you didn't answer my text the other night—"

"What text?" Natasha interrupted.

"I sent you a message after we got off the phone. You didn't answer me."

Natasha shook her head. "I didn't get it." Knowing Brick, he was drunk and thought he sent it but usually he didn't. It happened when he was drunk.

"Well, I sent it."

"It doesn't matter if you sent it or not because I am done. I told you; I can't do this anymore. You don't love me, and I need somebody in my life who loves me. Somebody who puts me first. Somebody who doesn't treat me like garbage."

"Somebody like Mason?" Brick grumbled.

Natasha rolled her eyes. "I am done having this argument with you. It's not like you listen to me, anyway. I told you; Mason has nothing to do with this. Or with us. Absolutely nothing."

"Now who's lying? Mason has always been smack-ass in the middle of our relationship. I've been competing with him for years." Brick threw himself back in his chair, a loud crack coming from it when he landed in it. "Whatever. I know you claim Mason has nothing to do with this, but I know better. Whether or not you want to admit it, you compare every guy you date to your brother's best friend. I don't compare to Mason."

"You never tried." Natasha snapped her mouth shut so fast she bit the tip of her tongue. She pinched the bridge of her nose and exhaled slowly. "It's over, Brick. I'm sorry. You believe whatever you want to believe. It doesn't matter anymore." She spun on her heel, hurried to the door, and yanked it open.

"You're a little bitch," Brick yelled after her. "I don't know why I ever thought I loved you."

Natasha froze for a split second, then she stepped out of the apartment and pulled the door closed behind her. Her fingers trembled as she took her apartment key off the ring and shoved it under the doormat. Once she was in her car, she took her phone out of her purse and blocked Brick's number. She prayed he would leave her alone.

She gripped the steering wheel hard as she drove to her brother's bar, cursing under her breath. How dare Brick say those things about Mason. Mason had nothing to do with the shit show her relationship with Jason "Brick" Brickman had become. Brick needed somebody to blame, and that somebody was Mason.

Speaking of Mason, she needed to talk to him. If Brick really had texted her, that meant Mason deleted it, which he had no right to do. She was going to make sure he knew it, too.

———

Natasha let the door slam shut behind her, stomped across the bar, and sat on the barstool next to Mason. She dropped her purse on the floor and laid her head on the bar with a sigh.

"How did it go?" Nate asked.

Her head came up, and she glared at her brother. "How do you think it went? It was a shit storm. He begged me to take him back. When I said no, he got pissed off and called me a bitch. He said a bunch of other stuff, too. He was an utter and complete ass."

"You went alone?" Mason interjected. "You should have told me you were going. I would have gone with you."

"You are the last person who should have gone with me," Natasha snapped. She hadn't meant to sound so bitchy, but frayed nerves did that to a person. She cleared her throat. Might as well get this over with. "Mace, did I get a text from Brick the other night? When you had my phone in your pocket?"

As soon as the question was out of her mouth, she knew she was right by Mason's reaction that there had been a text, a text she never saw. Mason's jaw tightened, and his fists clenched on the top of the bar. He opened his mouth, then snapped it shut again.

"Tash, I was just—."

"Trying to protect me?" she asked. "When are you and my brother going to figure out that I can take care of myself? I'm a big girl, an actual grown-up. I don't need your help."

"You were upset. I thought it would be best if you didn't talk to him anymore."

Natasha slapped her hand down on the bar. "That's my choice, Mason. Mine. Not yours. Not Nathaniel's. Mine and mine alone. I appreciate that you thought you were helping, but you can't make those kinds of decisions for me. Trust me to do it on my own."

Mason stared at the top of the bar, his face tight and pinched. "Okay. I'm sorry."

Nate reached across the bar and took her hands. "Nattie, don't be mad."

Natasha shook her head and tried not to smile. Nate using her hated childhood nickname wasn't going to lighten the moment or cheer her up.

"Don't call me that," she muttered. "It's Natasha or Tasha. Pick one." She sat up straight, her shoulders back. "Look, I'm fine. I promise. I just want to forget today happened." She straightened her shoulders and took a deep breath. "Nathaniel Boris Garin, I demand you get me a drink. A glass of wine. Or maybe a bottle."

Nate made a face at her, but he did as she asked. After a few drinks and some food, maybe she would feel better. At least, that's what she hoped.

—

Natasha dropped the pool cue on the table and threw her hands in the air. "Four in a row, baby!" she yelled. "Beat that!"

Mason laughed and shook his head. "You're on a roll. I'm not even going to try." He reached for his scotch and soda, but before he could pick it up, Natasha snatched it, downed the remainder, and slammed it down on the table.

"I need another drink!"

"Um, no, I think I need another drink." Mason snorted. "And maybe you should have some water."

Natasha made a face and shook her head. "I'm fine. In fact, maybe I'll have a margarita instead of another glass of wine. Where's my brother?" She spun around, grabbing the table to steady herself.

Mason took her elbow and helped her sit at one of the nearby tables. "You're done," he said.

"You're such a party pooper," she mumbled. "You know, I don't need you to babysit me. I can take care of myself."

"I know," Mason said. He sat down next to her and took her hand. "I'm just looking out for you. I've been looking out for you for twenty years."

Natasha sighed. "Maybe I'm sick of you looking out for me." She scrubbed a hand over her face. "I'm sorry; that was mean." She pushed herself to her feet, wobbling slightly. "I'm going to the ladies' room, and then I'm going home."

Mason grabbed her hand. "You're not driving, right?"

"Of course not. I'll call an Über or something."

"I can take you," he offered.

"No offense, Mace, but I really don't want you to take me home. I need a break. From you, from Nate, from everybody." She spun around, grabbing the table again to steady herself before stomping down the hall to the bathroom.

Natasha took a minute to splash some water on her face before she returned to the pool tables. Mason had a beer, and sitting on the table in front of her seat was a bottle of water. She dropped onto the stool, took a sip of her water, and cleared her throat.

"You can't drive me home. You've been drinking," she said, pointing at Mason's beer bottle.

"I know," he replied. "I called you an Über; it should be here any minute." He pushed her purse across the table with a smirk. "I'm not going. I'm going to stay here and help Nate. Go home and get some sleep. Take a break from both me and Nate, just like you asked."

Natasha snatched her purse off the table and stood up. "Goddamn you, Mason." She leaned over him, the spicy scent of his cologne assaulting her senses. She forced herself to concentrate, to get the words out. "You're too damn nice. I hate it."

Mason's phone lit up. He glanced at it. "Your Über is here." He scrubbed his mouth with the back of his hand and didn't meet her eyes. "I'll talk to you later. When you're sober."

Natasha rolled her eyes, yelled goodbye to her brother, and pushed through the crowd out the door. Tears stung her eyes, and her heart thumped erratically in her chest. She wanted to scream.

What the hell is wrong with me?

Chapter 8

Mason

Mason couldn't blame Natasha for being pissed. As usual, his attempts to protect her and watch out for her, like he'd always done, had resulted in him overstepping his bounds and making Natasha angry.

It's just like high school all over again.

Sophomore year of high school, Natasha dated a transfer student, a football player named Reggie. To Mason's unending irritation, Natasha was completely enamored with Reggie. Natasha always went for the jocks, something Mason wasn't, at least not in the tenth grade. They dated for weeks and seemed like a good match, at least according to everyone in school. Except for Mason, who knew they weren't. Natasha played a part when she was with Reggie, acting like someone she wasn't.

A month into their relationship, Mason saw Reggie in a downtown restaurant with a pretty brunette woman in a University of Montana sweatshirt. They seemed far too friendly to be friends.

Mason told Nate, and the two of them confronted Reggie. Reggie brushed them off and told them they were idiots for thinking he would cheat on Natasha. Mason kept pushing until Reggie blew up at him, screaming at him to back off. Mason took a swing, missed by a mile, and fell on his ass. Reggie laughed at him and walked away.

Mason went straight to Natasha, intent on breaking the news. To his chagrin, Natasha was furious with him. Reggie had already told her what happened; the girl Mason saw Reggie with was his cousin, visiting from college for the weekend. He felt like an idiot. Worse, Natasha was so angry, she refused to talk to him or Nate for weeks. She called them both overbearing and ridiculous.

Even after Natasha discovered the woman wasn't Reggie's cousin, but a former girlfriend, her anger with Mason didn't diminish. When Reggie broke up with her and started dating the former girlfriend, Natasha claimed it was because he couldn't deal with her brother and his best friend always being around.

This was too much like that. Mason knew Brick was the wrong guy for Natasha, but he couldn't convince her. Everyone knew Brick was an asshole, so why didn't Natasha know? Mason had her best interests in mind—always. He wanted to protect her, shield her from any harm or pain. He knew she could stand up for herself and take care of herself, but whenever he was around her, an overwhelming need to take care of her came over him.

After Natasha left, he switched to drinking water. It wasn't that he was drunk; he'd only had two drinks while he and Natasha played pool. But he wanted to drive home, so no more alcohol.

Business in the bar seemed to pick up during the last hour, so Mason slipped behind the counter to help Nate, taking over bartending duties while Nate bussed tables. Mason enjoyed helping Nate at the bar; he was good at it, and it was easy. Nate had been short-staffed off and on all summer, so Mason had helped several times when this happened. Hanging out at the bar allowed Natasha to get a much- needed break from both him and Nate at home, while it gave him a chance to think. It was easy to slip back into bartender mode; he could mix drinks in his sleep, and he enjoyed listening to the customers talk about their day.

It was after midnight when he finally left the bar. Nate had become preoccupied with one of his female customers, deciding to show her all his bartending tricks. Not wanting to be in the way, Mason said his goodbyes and took off.

He drove slowly through town toward home, taking his time. He wanted to talk to Natasha, but he wanted her to be sober. He had a feeling that wouldn't be tonight. She was probably out cold on the couch, as she'd had a lot more to drink than she normally did. So, Mason was in no rush to get home.

Their house was one of fifteen built on a small hill over-looking Lakeside. They'd been built to appeal to the married college students who came to Lakeside to attend the college, or those students not interested in dorm life. He and Nate moved into their house when they were in college, and neither of them saw a reason to move out after they graduated. It was a five-minute drive to Nate's bar and close to the photography studio where Mason worked. It was small but comfortable.

At least it had been when it was just the two of them; three people living there was a bit much. Nat liked to joke that they were like the three roommates on an old TV show his parents liked, *Three's Company*.

Mason parked in the empty driveway. He still felt bad about the text he'd deleted and wished he could take it back. He understood why Natasha was angry and hurt. If Mason could fix the situation, he would.

The lights were off in the house, and it was eerily quiet. If Mason hadn't sent her home in the Über, he would have thought Natasha wasn't there. He unlocked the door and stepped inside. Natasha wasn't asleep on the couch like he'd expected. Instead, he could see a light in the small backyard. He made his way through the house to the back door and slipped outside.

Natasha was on the steps at the end of the patio, hugging herself and staring down the hill at Flathead Lake. She had on his gray Lakeside College hoodie. It was huge on her; the sleeves hung down past her hands, and the bottom hem covered her thighs. Mason crossed the patio and sat down beside her.

"You know I've been looking for that sweatshirt," he said.

Natasha laughed quietly. "I took it weeks ago; it's comfy."

"It's okay," he whispered. He bumped his shoulder against hers. "Hi. I thought you'd be passed out on the couch."

"I guess I sobered up." She bumped into him like he'd done to her. "What are you doing home? I thought you were staying at the bar with Nate. You know, to give me space."

Mason chuckled. "The sarcasm is unnecessary. I came home. Nate was … preoccupied."

"A woman?"

"Yeah? Dottie? That's her name, right? Isn't she the one who was here a few nights ago?"

"I think so. Do you think it's serious?" she asked.

Mason snorted. "I doubt it. When was the last time Nate had a serious relationship?"

Natasha giggled. "Um, never." She shook her head. "I didn't realize my brother was such a ladies' man. It's kind of weird, you know. To me, he's just my annoying twin brother who drives me crazy. I don't see him as somebody women want to date. I guess I don't know him as well as I thought I did."

Mason exhaled loudly. "You haven't been around much the last few years, Tash. People change."

Natasha rolled her eyes. "That's not fair; I was around. You're just upset because I've been living my own life without you and Nate interfering."

Mason scoffed. "That's not true, and you know it. You spent the last two years doing everything in your power to stay away from us."

"Yeah, you're right, I did." Natasha put her head in her hands. "And look where it got me."

Mason slipped his arm around Natasha and hugged her. "I'm sorry. I shouldn't have said anything."

"No, no, you're right. If I hadn't tried so hard to prove to everyone that I wasn't just Nate's twin sister, that there was more to me than that, I might know more about my brother's life. Shit, I might know more about him. I'm not joking when I say I did not know so many women wanted to date him."

"*All* the women want to date your brother." Mason chuckled. "Especially the college girls."

"Ew."

"Sorry. It's true, though. I swear he has a new woman every week. I can't believe Dottie has been around for more than a week. In fact, it's miraculous. And it's not that you don't know him well; it's just that Nate lives his own life on his own terms."

Natasha snorted. "Yes, he does. Especially since Daddy helped him buy the bar. That place *is* his life."

Mason tapped a finger against his chin. "Maybe that's why he doesn't have time for a relationship. Owning the Time Out takes all his free time."

"He uses the bar as an excuse not to get too close to anyone," Natasha said. "As soon as they want more, he moves on. He blames it on the bar. My brother doesn't want to get close to anybody."

Mason shook his head. "Not true. Nate has a lot of friends; he has you, Oscar, Gavin, your parents—"

Natasha patted his leg. "He has you."

"Exactly. Maybe he hasn't found the right woman yet," Mason suggested. "It takes some people a while to find the one person they want to be with for the rest of their life."

Natasha laughed. "And some people are like me. They find someone and discover too late he's an asshole."

Mason cleared his throat. "I'm sorry, Tasha. About everything. I'm sorry Brick is an asshole, and I'm sorry I didn't let Nate kick his ass." He took her hand and held it tight. "And I'm really sorry for overstepping and deleting that text message. I shouldn't have done that. I wanted to protect you, but I should have known you knew what you were doing, and you can look out for yourself. Without my help. After twenty years, it's kind of force of habit to look out for you."

Natasha stared at the lake, illuminated by the moon, a frown on her face. "I can't say that I'm okay with what you did or that I'm not mad. I'm a big girl, Mace. I got myself into this mess with Brick, and I need to get myself out of it." She closed her eyes and pinched the bridge of her nose. "At least I hope I get myself out of it. I know you and my brother think you're helping, but I have to deal with this on my own. Brick is my problem." She shivered and wrapped her arms around herself.

Mason wrapped his arm around her and hugged her close, sharing his body heat.

"Why are you so nice to me, Mason Adler?" she whispered.

Because I've been in love with you since first grade.

Not that he said that out loud. Instead, Mason shrugged. "I don't know. I guess it's because you're my best friend's sister. And you're my friend. How could I not be nice to you?"

Natasha tensed and abruptly stood up.

"Do you have any hot chocolate in this place?" she asked.

"I don't know," Mason replied.

"Come on, let's go check the kitchen." She tipped her head toward the back door.

Mason nodded and stood up. He thought about taking Natasha's hand, but it wouldn't mean the same thing to her. Instead, he tucked his hands in the pockets of his jeans and followed Natasha inside.

Chapter 9
Natasha

Avery came through the door like a woman on a mission, her blonde curls flying behind her and a huge smile on her face. She kissed Natasha's cheek before she dropped into the seat across from her.

Avery and Natasha had been roommates during college, sharing an apartment off-campus. They hadn't been close at first, but as time went on, they'd become good friends. After Avery got involved with one of her professors—a man only a couple of years older than her—her world turned upside down. Fortunately, everything worked out in the end, but the ordeal had brought the two of them closer than ever.

"You look tired, Nat," she said. Avery was the only person besides Brick who called her Nat instead of Natasha or Tasha.

"Wow, hello to you, too," Natasha said.

Avery flinched and gave her friend a sheepish grin. "Sorry, sweetie. That was a pretty crappy greeting." She reached across the table and took Natasha's hand. "How are you?"

"I'm exhausted," Natasha replied.

Avery sat back, crossed her arms over her chest, and made a face. "I can't imagine why."

"Well, let's see." Natasha held up her hand and ticked off each point as she spoke. "I'm sleeping on a lumpy, uncomfortable couch. I'm living with two bachelors, one of whom is my brother, and the other is a guy I've known almost my entire life. My fiancé—sorry, ex-fiancé—cheated on me and is inexplicably pissed at *me* for breaking off the engagement. Oh, and my brain is a jumbled mess." Natasha took a sip of her coffee and shrugged.

"Understandable, after what Brick did," Avery said.

"It's not just Brick; it's Mason, too."

Avery's eyebrows shot up. "Mason? What the hell did Mason do?"

"Nothing specific. He's just being … well, he's just being Mason." Natasha pushed a hand through her hair. "He's so goddamn nice. Overbearingly nice. So much so that I hate it."

Avery laughed. "No, you don't. It might irk you a little, but you don't hate it. Mason's your friend, and a good one at that. What you hate is that he knows you better than you know yourself."

"No, he doesn't," Natasha snapped.

"Yes, he does," Avery insisted. "He's been part of your life for what, something like eighteen years?"

"More like twenty," Natasha said. "Since first grade. Mason has always been there, you know? Wherever Nate was, Mason was right there, too. They were inseparable."

"I seem to remember you telling me you and Nate were inseparable when you were kids. If he and Mason were always together, doesn't that mean *all* of you were always together?"

Natasha chewed on the inside of her mouth and glared at her friend. "Yes," she admitted begrudgingly.

Avery smiled and shook her head. "Quit pouting and hear me out. Mason is Nate's best friend, right? But don't you think he's your friend, too? Maybe not your best friend, but he's your friend."

"Yeah," Natasha said. "Mason's my friend. He's probably one of my best friends."

Avery cleared her throat. "Has it ever occurred to you that maybe Mason wants to be more than your friend?"

Natasha raised an eyebrow. "Excuse me?"

"Think about it, Nat," Avery said. "Try to see Mason as someone other than your old friend from school, the guy you grew up with who lived down the street."

Natasha rolled her eyes. "I've been friends with Mason forever. Don't you think I would have noticed if he had some weird crush on me?"

Avery picked up her coffee, sat back, and took a sip. "Honestly, Nat, no, I don't think you would notice."

"What's that supposed to mean?" Natasha snapped.

"Hey, hear me out," Avery said. "I'm not saying anything bad about you. All I'm saying is maybe Mason did a fantastic job of keeping his feelings for you under wraps. From what you've told me, you were popular in high school and Mason was ... not. Would you have dated him in high school?"

Natasha shook her head no. Not in a million years. Mason was her friend, but not her type at all. Back in high school, he'd been skinny, uncoordinated, nonathletic, and nerdy.

"And after high school, you kind of went your own way, right?"

"Yeah." The wheels spun in Natasha's head. *God, is Avery right? Is Mason harboring some long-standing crush on me?*

"Look, I'm just speculating here," Avery continued, "but maybe Mason is overbearingly nice for a reason." She shrugged. "It could be worth a conversation."

Natasha choked on her coffee and burst out laughing. "You think I should ask him? Wow, I can just hear that conversation. 'Hey, Mason, have you been harboring a super-secret crush on me for twenty years?' That's ridiculous, Avery."

Avery giggled. "You could start there."

"Okay, let's say he has had a crush on me. Then what?"

"Well, how do you feel about him?" Avery asked.

"What do you mean?"

"You heard me," Avery snapped. "How do you feel about Mason? Can you see yourself with him? Is there something there?"

"I just broke up with my fiancé, Avery!"

Avery rolled her eyes. "I know that, Nat. But that doesn't mean you're made of stone. You can't be completely oblivious to Mason. I mean, that man is desirable. *Hot.*"

Heat rushed to Natasha's cheeks. Avery was right; she wasn't oblivious to Mason or his looks. Or how incredibly sweet he could be. She closed her eyes and took a deep breath before she spoke.

"Okay, look, I have noticed how attractive Mason is. I'd have to be dead not to see it. Especially when he comes home after his run in that damn half-zipped sweatshirt, running shorts, and stupid man bun, all sweaty and breathing heavy. I'd be crazy not to notice. And maybe, just *maybe*, the fact that's he's so sweet bugs me because I actually like it. And I shouldn't."

"What do you mean you shouldn't?"

"Again, I just broke up with my fiancé. It's a little too soon to be swooning over some guy."

Avery reached across the table and squeezed Natasha's hands. "He isn't some guy, Nat; he's Mason."

"Yeah," Natasha whispered. "Or maybe the problem is, *he's Mason*. I've known him my whole life. Where's the excitement, the thrill of something—someone—new? Figuring out what they like, what they want, who you can be to them? Where's all that?"

"Maybe that's the thing. It might be nice to be with someone who knows you. Someone you don't have to pretend with or figure out. Someone who likes you for you, faults and all," Avery said. "Talk to him."

Natasha shook her head. "I don't know if I can. I mean, I'm not even sure Mason has feelings for me or that he wants to date me. This is all speculation. Mason has never said or done anything that makes me think he is interested in anything more than friendship. I thought we had a moment the other night. We were really opening up to each other, and there were these feelings bouncing around in the air between us, but then he told me he's nice to me because I'm Nate's sister."

"What? You're kidding, right?"

"I wish," Natasha said. "But it's true."

"You're not going to say anything to him, are you?" Avery asked.

Natasha shook her head. "I can't, Avery. I'm not in a good place right now. I don't think I could handle it if Mason rejected me. After everything I've been through the last few weeks, something like that would push me right over the edge."

Avery sighed, but she nodded. "I get it; I do. But my advice is still to talk to him. Ask him. Tell him you deserve to know how he feels. Once you know for sure, then you can decide what you're going to do. And I shouldn't have to tell you this, but if you need someone to talk to, I'm a phone call away."

Natasha sipped her lukewarm coffee and smiled at her friend. "Thank you. I can't tell you how much I appreciate that. Now, enough about me and my lousy life. Tell me how Jacob is, and how your new job is going."

A huge smile spread across Avery's face, and she immediately launched into a story about her new job and life with her professor, Jacob. Natasha listened, trying to smile and nod in the appropriate places as she sipped her coffee.

At least somebody is happy.

—

Natasha threw her backpack under the table and pushed the door closed behind her. Nate was on the couch with a pretty blonde snuggled up against him; Natasha wondered if it was Dottie. Mason was at the other end of the couch, as far away from the affectionate couple as possible. Open beer bottles and several bowls of popcorn sat on the table in front of them.

Mason turned to look at her, a desperate grin on his face. "Tasha! You're home."

"I am." She kicked off her shoes and tossed her coat on the chair beside her backpack.

"Come sit by me," Mason begged. He stared at her with puppy-dog eyes, blinking rapidly. She had to stifle a giggle.

"What are we doing tonight?" she asked.

"We're watching a movie!" Nate said. "Come watch it with us."

Natasha froze in place, then she spun around, with her hands on her hips. "As long as it's not a romantic comedy. I am not in the mood for any kind of rom-com. Actually, I'm not in the mood for *any* kind of romance." She glared at her brother and his best friend before she went into the bathroom and slammed the door.

She couldn't tolerate some cheesy romance, not with the mood she was currently in. Her head spun like crazy since she left Avery; she was equal parts angry and sad about the turn her life had taken. A month ago, she wouldn't have pictured herself where she was—no fiancé, sleeping on her brother's couch, and suddenly unsure of what her feelings for Mason were. This was all Avery's fault.

Natasha splashed cold water on her cheeks and changed into the sweatpants and t-shirt she kept stashed in the bathroom cupboard. After taking a few deep breaths and centering herself, she returned to the living room and headed for the kitchen.

The girl who had been sitting on the couch with Nate had her head in the refrigerator. She straightened up when Natasha entered the kitchen.

"Hi there," she said. "I'm Dottie." She stuck out her hand.

Natasha shook the girl's hand. "Hello. I'm Natasha. I'm Nate's sister."

Dottie bit into a piece of celery; her answer came around the crunch of celery in her mouth. "It's so great to meet you. Nate talks about you all the time. I heard about what happened between you and your boyfriend. I'm really sorry."

Natasha smiled stiffly. "Thanks." She cleared her throat. "Do you mind if I get in there?" She pointed at the fridge.

"Oh, yeah, sorry." Dottie stepped out of the way. "I'm done, anyway. I'll see you in the living room."

Natasha grabbed a bottle of water, took a deep breath, and went to join everyone else on the couch.

"So, what are we watching?" she asked.

"A horror movie," Nate said.

"I hate horror movies." She sat down next to Mason, her leg pressed against his, as she scooped a handful of popcorn from the bowl on his lap and shoved it in her mouth. Cued up and ready to play on the TV was the latest popular horror movie.

Nate and Mason both laughed. "You do not," Nate said. "You love them."

"Can't we watch another baseball game or something? That was fun when we did that the other night."

"There isn't a game on tonight, unless we want to watch the Yankees," Nate said.

"Yuck," Mason interjected.

Natasha noticed Mason avoided eye contact with her. Things had been awkward between them since the night they'd sat on the back porch and talked. Natasha did not know how or why things had gotten so weird, and she hated it. She wanted to fix it, but she didn't know how.

"There you go. No baseball games, little sister says no romance movies, so horror movie it is!" Nate grinned and hit play.

Natasha grabbed the blanket off the back of the couch and pulled it over her lap. She prayed the movie wouldn't be too scary. At first, it wasn't so bad; the movie depended on the jump scare tactic. She got through the first couple of scary parts without losing it, but when the set of hands came out of nowhere and clapped next to the mother's head, she lost it. A loud scream escaped her, and she hid her face against Mason's shoulder.

He tried to scoot away from her, but there was nowhere for him to go. Natasha wrapped her arms around him and inched closer to him.

"Get back here," she whispered. "You need to protect me."

Mason laughed, slid his arm around her waist, and put his hand on her hip. Natasha snuggled closer, the blanket clutched in her hands, pulled up next to her face. If anybody in the world could protect her, it was Mason.

Chapter 10

Natasha

Natasha laid awake after everyone else had gone to bed. Every few minutes, a ridiculous giggle would erupt from Nate's room. The thought of what might be going on behind Nate's bedroom door made her gag.

She rolled to her side, punched one of her two pillows a few times, and laid back down with the other pillow over her head. She stared at Mason's closed door and the dim light emanating from the crack at the bottom. He was still awake.

When had her world turned upside down? How did a guy she considered a friend suddenly become something more in her eyes? Was this a rebound thing, her heart screaming at her to find someone new to heal the deep fissure in her chest? Or were these new, bizarre feelings a product of Avery's suggestions? Who knew?

Natasha could make up all kinds of excuses for why she shouldn't get involved with Mason, why a relationship with him was a bad idea. Not that any of those reasons occurred to her as she laid on the couch, staring at his door.

Maybe it wasn't a bad idea. Mason was sweet, protective, and, of course, gorgeous. She could definitely do worse.

Another giggle, this one louder than the others, came from her brother's room. She pressed the pillow tight against her head, squeezed her eyes closed, and tried not to listen.

When Mason's bedroom door opened, Natasha's eyes popped open. She watched him tiptoe across the room, headed for the kitchen. He wore nothing but a pair of gray sweatpants, hung low on his hips; his feet were bare, as was his chest. Natasha dragged in a deep breath and let it out slowly, as she watched his delectable ass cross the room.

Delectable ass? What the hell?

She tossed the pillow to the end of the couch, threw off her blanket, and followed Mason to the kitchen. He had his head in the refrigerator and mumbled to himself.

"Hey, Mace," she whispered.

Mason jumped, his head connecting with the refrigerator, a quiet curse leaving him. He stood upright and rubbed his head.

"I thought you were asleep," he muttered.

As if on cue, another giggle came from Nate's room. Natasha pointed at her brother's door. "Who can sleep with that going on?"

Mason chuckled. "I can't hear it in my room."

"Lucky," Natasha mumbled. "I've been listening to it for an hour. I can't sleep."

Mason shifted from foot to foot and cleared his throat. "If you want, you could crash in my room; you can't hear anything in there. I'll throw my sleeping bag on the floor, and you can have the bed."

"I don't want to put you out—"

"You're not."

Natasha made a face, prompting Mason to shake his head and laugh.

"I swear. It's fine." He grabbed a bottle of water from the fridge and pushed the door shut with his knee. "Come on."

Natasha considered saying no, but the promise of a good—or at least decent—night's sleep beckoned. She followed Mason to his room. He threw his sleeping bag and pillow on the floor and pointed at the bed for her.

"I just changed the sheets yesterday, and there's an extra pillow you can use."

"Thanks." She shut the door, dropped to the bed, and pulled the blankets up to her chin. The scent of Mason surrounded her—leather and amber. He'd been wearing the same cologne since high school; any time she smelled it, she thought of him.

Natasha stared at the ceiling and tried to work up the nerve to talk to Mason about what she was feeling and, more importantly, how he felt about her. She wasn't sure she could sleep until they talked.

Talk to him.

She hated that tiny voice in her head, but it was right. So was Avery. If she was truly developing feelings for Mason, and maybe vice versa, they needed to get it out in the open and be honest with each other.

The truth will set us free.

She peered over the side of the bed. Mason was on his back, his long black hair spread out across the pillow, one hand resting on his stomach. Light snores were coming from his open mouth.

"Dammit," she muttered. The truth would have to wait for another day.

Natasha straightened out the blankets, adjusted the pillow under her head, and closed her eyes. As she drifted off to sleep, she promised herself she would talk to Mason sooner rather than later.

She slept better than she expected, straight through until the sun came up. Mason was gone when she woke up, but her brother was on the couch, arms crossed and staring at her as she emerged from Mason's room.

"Is there something you want to tell me?" Nate demanded.

Natasha rolled her eyes. "No. Mason slept on the floor, and I slept in his bed. He was kind enough to let me crash in his room because listening to my brother's latest conquest giggling all night made me nauseous."

Nathaniel had the good sense to look embarrassed. "Oh, god, I'm sorry," he whispered. He jumped off the couch and hugged his sister. "I swear I didn't mean to traumatize you."

"You're forgiven," she said. "Just try to rein it—and her—in, please."

"I will, I promise." Nate kissed her cheek. "Now that I have my explanation why you're in Mason's room, I can go to work. See you tonight."

———

The next few weeks were a blur. Natasha's vow to talk to Mason about his feelings—and hers—was far more elusive than she imagined. She couldn't seem to get a minute alone with him, despite every effort to get him by himself.

If he wasn't working, she was. His calendar was full of photo shoot after photo shoot, and when he wasn't doing that, his part-time job as an EMT at the small Lakeside hospital kept him busy, especially during summer. He'd gone from working two days a week to three days a week; it seemed more like a full-time job than something he did as a side job. Mason also stepped in to help Nate whenever he was short-staffed at the bar, which seemed to be several times a week.

As for Natasha, rehearsals for the theater's summer show were in full swing. Not only was she the theater manager, co-director, stage manager, and head of marketing, but she also had a part in the show. She did the menial work during the day and ran rehearsals at night. Most nights, she didn't get home until close to midnight and by then, Mason was sound asleep. If he wasn't home, he was at the bar, and she was asleep by the time he got home. Their lives were a revolving door of schedules.

Two weeks before the show's opening night, Natasha had a rare night off. Instead of going home like she should have, she stopped at the Time Out Bar and Grill to see her brother. As crazy as he made her, he was still her brother—her twin brother—and whether she wanted to admit it or not, she needed him. Maybe he could help her figure out a way to talk to Mason.

Of course, that meant telling Nate she might be developing feelings for his best friend. While she suspected her brother probably already knew—she could hide nothing from him—coming right out and telling him was a little scary. He could react one of two ways: utter, total, and complete anger, or he would love the idea. Natasha hoped for the latter.

She parked her car on the street and took a deep breath. The bar didn't look too crowded; the lot was close to empty, with only seven or eight cars parked with hers. She grabbed her purse and headed inside.

Natasha was right; the bar wasn't crowded. Most of the cars must have belonged to the staff. Nate was behind the bar, where he always was, chatting with a woman, of course. He waved when he saw his sister and gestured for her to join him.

"Hey Tash, you want a drink?" he asked when she sat down.

"Just water. With lemon."

Nate rolled his eyes, but he did as she asked.

"Am I interrupting anything?" Natasha whispered, tipping her head in the direction of the woman Nate had been talking to.

Nate laughed and shook his head. "No. Cecily's a friend. Things have been rough for her lately, and she needed someone to talk to."

"She's not one of your many conquests?" Natasha winked.

"Uh, no." Nate cleared his throat. "What are you doing here in the middle of the afternoon? No rehearsal?"

"No." She traced the rim of her water glass and contemplated how she would tell her brother about Mason.

Somehow Nate knew; he always knew. He leaned on the bar, took his sister's hand, and squeezed it. "Talk to me, Natasha Anne. What's going on? Is it Brick?"

Natasha bit her lip and shook her head. "Is there someplace quiet we can talk? Your office, maybe?"

"Come on." Nate tossed his rag in the sink, stopped to whisper something in one of the server's ears, and then slipped out from behind the bar.

Natasha followed him down the hall and up a short staircase to a small office tucked under the eaves at the front of the bar. He sat behind his desk, and she took a seat on the old recliner across from him.

"Okay, sis. What did you want to talk about?"

"Mason."

Nate grimaced. "I know it's hard living with two bachelors, but we're doing our best, I swear. Mason is having a hard time adjusting to you being around all the time, that's all."

"That's not what I'm talking about. Yes, living with a couple of bachelors sucks, but I'm getting used to it." Natasha took a deep breath. "Mason has been our friend for a long time."

Nate crossed his arms over his chest and raised an eyebrow. "Stop beating around the bush, Tash. What the hell is going on? Did Mason do something I should be concerned about?"

Natasha shook her head. "No. It's not anything like that."

"Then spit it out."

"I think ... I think I like Mason," Natasha blurted.

Nate was silent for far too long. When he finally spoke, there was a gleeful quality to his voice that threw Natasha out of whack.

"You like Mason? Like, you like, *like* Mason? As in, like him more than a friend, maybe like him like a boyfriend?"

"Could you say 'like' a few more times, please?" Natasha muttered. Nate just smirked at her. "Yes, I have feelings for Mason. At least, I think I do."

"You either do or you don't, Tash. I don't think there is really an in-between."

Natasha squeezed her eyes shut. "Except right now, I'm not sure how I feel. Mason is my friend, and he's been looking out for me. I'm noticing him in ways I never did before. But—"

Nate sighed. "There is always a 'but.'"

"But I just broke up with Brick. Those wounds are still fresh. So, yes, I might have feelings for Mason, but I'm not sure what to do about them."

Nate leaned forward and stared into his sister's eyes. He looked so serious she wanted to laugh. "Have you told Mason?" he asked.

"You sound like Avery," she mumbled.

"Have you?" Nate pressed.

"No, I haven't told him. I'm not even sure what to say." Natasha threw her head back against the recliner and groaned. "What am I gonna do?"

"You know what Mom says," Nate said. "Sometimes you have to do something you hate to know what you really want."

"Don't quote our mother at me," Natasha grumbled. "If I want a lecture, I'll call home."

Nate laughed. "Sorry. But sometimes our mother knows what she's talking about."

Natasha stuck her tongue out at him. "You didn't answer my question. What am I gonna do?"

Nate sighed, sat back, and crossed his arms over his chest. "Tell him, Tasha. He deserves to know."

Natasha sat back and crossed her arms over her chest, mimicking her brother. "Why doesn't this bother you? I thought you'd lose your mind when I told you. You're surprisingly calm."

"I guess because it doesn't surprise me." Nate scrubbed a hand over his face. "And maybe I like the idea of you and Mason together. He's a great guy, and you're my sister." He leaned forward, his elbows on his desk, gazing intently at her. "He'd be good for you, Tash. You'd be good together."

"You think so?" she asked.

Nate nodded.

"Okay, great. How do you feel about talking to him about me?" She gave him her best sisterly smile. "Pretty please?"

"What is this, high school?" Nate chuckled. "I don't think I should talk to him. He needs to hear it from you. Not me."

Natasha slumped in her seat and put her hand over her eyes. "I know, I know. I just need to find the right time."

"There's never a right time," Nate said. "Get him alone and tell him."

"Or you will?" Natasha asked hopefully.

"Um, no." Nate shook his head and pointed at her. "That's up to you, my darling sister."

———

Easier said than done.

Getting Mason alone didn't get any easier after telling Nate about her feelings for his best friend. She didn't know why she thought it would.

"Earth to Tasha?"

"Hm?"

Nate shook his head and sighed. "I asked if you talked to Mason yet?"

"I'm trying, okay? Besides, it's only been a few days since I told you. I just can't seem to get him alone. Every time I try, something happens—people showing up to watch baseball on the big screen, Mason getting called into work, a costume emergency at the theater. It's a never-ending stream of craziness around this place."

"He's going to be home tonight, and I'm going to be at work. I'm closing, so I won't be home until two or three in the morning. There's no baseball game, no distractions. Unless he gets called into the hospital, he'll be here. Talk to him tonight."

Natasha exhaled. "I can do that. At least I think I can."

Nate laughed. "Don't think about it; do it." He kissed the top of his sister's head. "I gotta go. Let me know how it goes." He grabbed his car keys and yelled goodbye over his shoulder.

Natasha got ready for rehearsal, determined to get home on time for once. She was out the door ten minutes early and had everything set up and ready to go by the time the other actors arrived. She ran rehearsal like a drill sergeant, keeping everyone moving, stopping only when necessary.

It felt good and, to her surprise, no one complained. In fact, when she called it a night, several of the other actors thanked her for a well-run rehearsal and getting them home early. Natasha drove home with a smile on her face about the compliments.

When she pulled into the driveway, Mason's truck was there. Natasha took a deep breath, grabbed her backpack, and climbed out of her car.

I can do this.

Chapter 11

Mason

Since the night of the horror movie, the inadvertent cuddling on the couch, and Natasha sleeping in his bed, she had acted weird every time the two of them were together. Mason kept hoping they could get a minute alone to talk, but it seemed like they were never by themselves.

A lot of that was his fault. He was swamped: weddings, family photos, and his part-time job as an EMT at the hospital kept him insanely busy. He'd even helped Nate at the bar a few times when he was short-staffed.

Maybe you're avoiding her.

"I'm not," he said out loud. He had officially lost it, talking out loud to himself. He'd gone off the deep end.

The sun hovered over Flathead Lake as Mason turned the corner and swung into the driveway. No one else was home; Nate was at the bar, and Natasha probably had theater rehearsal. He wasn't sure if he should be relieved or not. He knew he needed to talk to Natasha, but the thought terrified him.

It wasn't Natasha he was afraid of; it was the rejection. He'd known this woman almost her whole life, and he had been in love with her for years. A rejection from the perfect woman, the only woman who had ever mattered to him, would be devastating.

No other woman compared to Natasha. None of the girls he dated in high school held a candle to her. Not even Allison—a woman he thought he loved—could withstand a comparison to Natasha. Allison always fell short because Natasha was the standard he held all women to because in his eyes, she was perfection.

Once Allison discovered this painful truth, it was over between them. It was an ugly breakup: screaming, yelling, throwing things, and accusations he couldn't deny. He did his best to smooth things over, but there was no appeasing Allison. Mason broke her heart, and, in return, she verbally eviscerated him. He deserved every word and took it all to heart. He was a coward and an asshole who led on a beautiful woman, hurt her, and destroyed her. The guilt still lingered two years later.

Exhausted after working sixteen hours straight, Mason let these thoughts wash over him as he moved through the house on autopilot. They weighed him down, souring his mood. He showered and ate something, then threw himself on the couch, propped his feet on the coffee table, and let those depressing thoughts follow him into sleep.

Nightmarish, vague dreams about Allison and Natasha haunted him. The front door opening and the kitchen light coming on dragged him out of a restless sleep. He had no idea what time it was. He grunted as he pushed himself upright.

"Hello?" Natasha called.

"Hey," he responded groggily. "I'm in here, on the couch."

Natasha stepped into the living room and hit the lights. "What are you doing sitting in the dark?" she asked.

Mason grunted and covered his eyes with his forearm. "I fell asleep." He checked his watch, surprised to see it was only a little after ten. "You're home early."

"Rehearsal wrapped early." She took a deep breath and gazed at him. "Can we talk for a minute?"

Mason straightened up. "Uh oh, this sounds serious."

Natasha giggled, but it was shaky and off-kilter, not her usual carefree and calm giggle. Mason's stomach did a slow roll as Natasha sat down next to him.

"This is so stupid," she muttered. "I don't know where to start. Shit, I don't know what to say."

"You know you can tell me anything," Mason said. "What is it?"

Natasha visibly swallowed. "Have you ever had a friend that was more than a friend? Or maybe you wanted them to be more than a friend?"

Mason chuckled. "Oh, yeah." *I'm looking at her.*

"Did you tell them?"

He shook his head. "No, I didn't." He leaned forward. "What are you trying to tell me, Tash?"

Mason's heart pounded so hard, it hurt. What the hell was this? What was happening?

Natasha gnawed on her lower lip and looked up at him through her eyelashes. She took a deep breath and opened her mouth, but before she could speak, someone pounded loudly on the front door.

"Dammit," Natasha muttered. She shoved herself to her feet and headed for the door, but Mason caught her hand in his, stopping her.

"I got it," he said. Mason walked to the door, with Natasha right behind him. He yanked it open and came face to face with Brick, reeking of cigarettes and alcohol. He swayed from side to side and blinked rapidly as he looked up at Mason.

"What the hell are you doing here?" Brick slurred.

"I live here, asshole," Mason snapped. "What are *you* doing here?"

"I came to talk to my fiancée," Brick replied. "Get the hell out of my way."

"I'm not your fiancée anymore, Brick," Natasha piped up. She stepped out from behind Mason. "Go away."

Brick put one foot over the threshold and reached for Natasha, but Mason pushed her out of the way, stepped in front of Brick, and stuck out his arm, blocking the doorway. "No one invited you in. I suggest you leave."

Brick grunted, put his hands on Mason's chest, and shoved as hard as he could. While Brick was stocky and, at one time, strong, he was no match for Mason, who stood 6' 6" and weighed 250. He towered over Brick by at least five inches and didn't even stumble when Brick pushed him.

Mason spread his legs and set his feet. "I said it was time for you to leave," he repeated.

Brick narrowed his eyes. "You know what, Adler? Fuck off." He stepped to the left to get around Mason but when Mason reached for him, Brick ducked and squeezed under Mason's outstretched arm, elbowing him in the gut as he passed him. Brick lunged at Natasha, who tried to back away, but Brick grabbed her arm, and yanked her close. "We need to talk. Now."

Natasha tried to yank her arm free, but Brick tightened his grip, his fingers sinking into the flesh of her upper arm. A startled gasp left her.

Mason had seen enough. He grabbed Brick by the back of the neck and squeezed. "Let her go."

Brick released Natasha with a growl and swung at Mason, his fist grazing Mason's chin. It didn't hurt, but it startled Mason, causing him to lose his grip and stumble back two steps. Brick yelled and leaped at Mason, throwing himself against the larger man's chest, his body weight sending them both to the floor.

They grappled with each other while Natasha stood over them, yelling at them to stop. Mason finally shoved Brick off and onto the floor, but not before Brick landed several blows to Mason's face and chest. Once Mason could get his feet under him, he grabbed Brick by the back of the shirt and half-carried, half-pulled Brick out the front door. He threw him onto the gravel driveway.

"Get out of here. Now," Mason ordered. "If you ever touch Tasha again, I'll put you in the hospital. Stay away from her; I mean it."

Brick touched a finger to his bleeding lip and winced. He shook his head and staggered to his feet. "This isn't over."

"Oh, but it is," Mason said. "I promise you, if you come back, you will regret it." He turned his back on Brick and went back into the house. He slammed the door behind him and stood at the window until Brick got in his car and drove off.

"Tasha, call Sheriff Willis and tell her Brick is driving drunk through downtown. I don't want anyone to get hurt."

—

An hour later, after a visit from Sheriff Willis, a frantic phone call from Nate, and one melted ice pack on his rapidly swelling eye, Mason and Natasha were finally alone. Again.

Mason laid on the couch, a bag of frozen peas on his eye, his head propped on a pillow. Natasha sat down beside him and brushed his hair out of his face.

"Thank you," she said.

"You're welcome," he whispered.

"I was, uh, gonna tell you something before we were rudely interrupted," she said.

"Oh, yeah, I almost forgot." He took the frozen peas off his eye and dropped it on the coffee table. "So, what exactly were you going to tell me?"

Natasha took his hand and stared at his fingers as she spoke. "You've always been there for me, Mason. You were the best friend I didn't know I had. Today proved that even more. Standing up to Brick like that—."

"Brick doesn't get to hurt you and get away with it." Mason looked down and whispered, "Nobody gets to hurt you and get away with it."

Natasha sighed and smiled. "Why are you such a good guy?"

Mason shrugged one shoulder and chuckled. "Thank my mom for raising me right."

Natasha laughed. "Trust me, I will next time I talk to her."

"You're stalling, Tash."

Natasha rolled her eyes. "Okay, fine." She exhaled and blurted, "Lately, I've been thinking that I might be ... well,

I guess what I'm trying to say is that I've been feeling like you and I could be more than friends."

"What?"

She pulled her hand out of his and punched him on the shoulder. "You heard me."

Mason put his hand on Natasha's hip and pulled her close. "Are you telling me you have feelings for me? Real, honest-to-God feelings?"

Natasha nodded. "Y-yes," she stammered. "At least, I think I do. I can't fight them anymore." She made a face, and all Mason wanted to do was kiss her.

He swallowed, licked his dry lips, and tried to control his shaking hands. Natasha could probably feel the tremor where his hand rested on her hip. He pushed himself upright, stared into Natasha's stormy gray eyes, and squeezed her ice-cold hand.

"What do you think we should do about it?" he whispered.

"I guess that's what we have to figure out, huh?" she murmured.

The front door flew open and slammed into the wall. "I'm going to kick Brick's ass!" Nate shouted as he walked through the house entrance.

Natasha shook her head, mouthed "sorry" and pushed herself to her feet. She turned to her brother. "No need, big brother. Mason already did."

Mason also stood up behind her, put his hand in the middle of Natasha's back, and whispered in her ear. "This isn't over, Tash. We have a lot to talk about."

"I know. And we will talk, I promise." She turned around, stood on her tiptoes, and kissed his cheek before hurrying across the room to meet her enraged brother.

Chapter 12
Natasha

A week after finally telling Mason how she felt about him, Natasha gave everyone at the theater a night off. They had been working hard and, with only a week and a half until the show, they deserved a day off. Of course, she still went to work; her job never seemed to end. She worked on the pile of paperwork she'd been neglecting, reached out to the local paper about advertising the show, and did some work on the theater's website. Giving everyone the night off was a great idea; not only was she grateful for the chance to get her neglected work done, but the prospect of a night off had her smiling all afternoon. Maybe she and Mason could finally talk about their feelings for each other.

On the way home, she stopped at the store and bought chicken, potatoes, and a salad. Before she moved in with Nate and Mason, it was unlikely a salad had ever crossed the threshold of the boys' small house. The thing she hated most about living with two bachelors—aside from sleeping on the couch and sharing a bathroom with two boys—was the lack of decent food in the house; it drove her crazy. A person could only eat so much cereal, frozen burritos, and Pop-tarts. If they weren't eating some kind of frozen food, they ate at the bar or got takeout—pizza, Chinese, or sandwiches from the deli. Natasha wanted actual food, and the only way to get it would be to cook it herself.

Once she was home, she dropped everything in the kitchen, changed into shorts and a t-shirt, put her headphones in, and went to work. Natasha danced around the kitchen barefoot while she cooked, lost in her own world.

Since she was intent on finishing the food preparation before Mason and Nate got home, she let herself get completely absorbed in what she was doing and, thanks to the music blasting in her ears, didn't hear the front door open and close. When a hand landed on her shoulder, she screamed and dropped the bottle of salad dressing in her hand. The plastic bottle bounced across the kitchen floor and slid to a stop beside the stove. She ripped the earbuds from her ears and spun around to yell at whoever scared the shit out of her.

Mason stood behind her, his hand pressed to his mouth in a poor attempt to stifle his laughter. His entire body shook, his face turned red, and tears formed at the corner of his eyes. He gulped and let out a laugh so loud, Natasha's eardrums vibrated.

She raised her hand to punch him, but Mason grabbed her wrist and held it comfortably tight. He took a step closer to her and trapped her between his rock-hard body and the kitchen counter. The jerk wasn't wearing a shirt, just that damn hoodie, unzipped to show off his chest, glistening with sweat. Her fingers itched to touch him, to flatten her hands on his chest and kiss him. Her entire body trembled at the thought.

Mason towered over her, staring down at her with his silvery-gray eyes. His tongue swiped across his lower lip. He released her wrist and put his hand on her waist, his fingers digging into her hip as he leaned over her.

"I think you owe me a kiss."

Time slowed; every second seemed to stretch into a minute as Mason moved closer. Anticipation heightened every sense, and longing twisted in her gut.

"I smell food!" her brother yelled, as he burst through the front door. "What's for dinner?"

Mason released her, shrugged, turned around, and made his way through the house, mumbling, "Hey, Nate," in his best friend's direction before he ducked into his bedroom.

"Shit," Natasha grumbled. She shot a death glare at Nate's back before she went back to making the salad. Her brother had impeccable timing. For the second time in a week, he had interrupted an important moment between her and Mason. She might kill him if he did it again.

—

After dinner, Nate left to pick up Dottie. Natasha sat on the couch and propped her feet on Mason's lap, who had been sitting there for a while. "What are you watching?"

"A World War II documentary." He glanced at her feet but didn't ask her to move them.

"That sounds boring," she mumbled.

"It's not boring," he scoffed. "The history of our world is interesting."

"I don't know why you didn't become a history teacher. You have an unusual obsession with world history." Natasha leaned over, plucked the water bottle from his hand, and took a drink.

"I didn't want to be a teacher," Mason replied.

"I know. Photography is your first love. But how fulfilling is it running someone else's photography studio in tiny little Lakeside, Montana? Senior pictures, the occasional wedding, family photos? Don't you want more?"

Mason made a face and shrugged. "I like my job. I like the studio. It frees me up to take photos of the things I really love: Flathead Lake, Glacier Park, the mountains, all of it. I love it here. The unique beauty of this place is like no other. I might like history, but I think teaching would bore me to tears. I enjoy having the freedom to pursue my art."

Natasha nodded. "I get that; it's why I love working for the theater. I may have to do the mundane, managerial stuff, but I get to do what I love. I get to be an actor." She took another drink of Mason's water and handed it back to him. "Hey, how come you've never taken any pictures of me?"

The look of surprise on Mason's face made her laugh. He opened his mouth and quickly closed it again. He contemplated his answer before he said, "I mean, I have taken pictures of you. I probably have hundreds of pictures of you."

"Yeah, but I don't think we've ever done an actual photoshoot, have we?"

Mason frowned and stared off into space, his usual look when he was thinking way too hard. "I, uh, I don't know. Do you want me to photograph you?"

Natasha shrugged. "I need new headshots, and I'd love to have you take them. I mean, I've been meaning to ask you, but I kept putting it off."

Mason tipped his head to one side and raised his eyebrow. She hated it when he did that; it gave him this sexy, smirky look that made goosebumps rise on her skin.

She bit her lip and stared back at him. "What?"

"Why'd you put it off?"

She resisted the urge to squirm under Mason's scrutiny. She gave him what she hoped was a nonchalant smile. "I didn't want to bug you. You have better things to do."

Mason looked skeptical, but he seemed to accept her answer. "I would love to photograph you. Figure out a day that works for you, and I'll take them."

"Okay, I will." Natasha cleared her throat and reached for the remote sitting on the couch between them. "Let's watch something else."

Mason snatched up the remote before she could grab it and held it over his head, out of her reach. Natasha lunged for it, threw herself across Mason's lap, and stretched as she tried to get it out of his hand. He switched it to the other hand and twisted away from Natasha to keep it away from her. He slid to the edge of the couch as she struggled to climb over him. They both fell to the floor, with Mason landing on top of her.

"Oof, get off of me, you giant."

Mason shrugged. "Hey, you started it."

She giggled and plucked the remote out of his hand. "Yes, I did. And thank you."

"Oh, okay, I see how it's going to be." He chuckled and shook his head. "All right, you asked for it."

He slid his hands up her sides, just below her ribs, and tickled her. He tickled her until she squealed and squirmed, her arms flailing and her legs kicking. He didn't stop until tears fell from her eyes, and she begged him to stop.

"Give me the remote," he whispered.

Mason was so close that the tip of his nose touched hers and their breath mingled. Natasha licked her lips, put her hands around the back of his neck, lifted her head, and brushed her lips against his.

Mason's eyes widened. He stiffened and attempted to shift his body away from hers. When Natasha urged him closer, tightening her grip on the back of his neck and tugging him down, Mason slipped his arm under her and relaxed against her, his hips nestled between her legs. He kissed her, tentatively at first, in a slow and easy manner. Natasha sighed and pressed her hand against the small of his back. As the kiss deepened, the world around her faded into the background until the only thing was Mason and the kiss; it was the single most perfect kiss she ever experienced.

When it was over—far sooner than Natasha wanted—Mason rested his forehead against hers and exhaled.

"Was that okay?" he whispered. His lips slid up her jaw to her ear.

"It was perfect." She tangled her fingers in his hair, turned her head toward him, and caught his lips in another kiss. "Absolutely perfect." She wanted to stay in his arms all night, as the thought of all the things they could do made her blood boil.

If Natasha hadn't heard the familiar sound of her brother's laughter outside the front door, she would have stayed wrapped in Mason's arms all night. Instead, the sound of raucous laughter and high-pitched giggles echoed through the night air.

Mason groaned. "Shit, Nate's back with Dottie." He released Natasha and climbed to his feet. Then he leaned over, effortlessly picked her up, and set her on the couch. Before they separated, he gave her a quick peck on the lips.

Nate came through the door with Dottie on his arm. When he saw his best friend and his sister in the living room, a cheesy grin contorted his handsome face into a clown-like caricature.

"Hey, guys," Nate said. "Whatcha doing?"

"Just watching some TV while we waited for you to get back," Mason said. "I was ... uh, gonna grab us some more beers. Do you guys want one?"

"Yeah, that sounds great!" Dottie piped up. "Doesn't it, Nate?" She gave Natasha's twin a flirty smile.

Nate shrugged. "I guess so." He kissed Dottie's cheek. "Wait here, babe. I'll help Mace with the beers and grab us some snacks."

"Get me a glass of wine!" Natasha yelled after her brother.

Dottie dropped to the couch beside Natasha. "Hey Tash, how's it going?"

Natasha forced herself to grin at the overly exuberant girl and her casual use of Natasha's nickname. "I'm doing well," she replied. "How have you been?"

"Great." Dottie smiled. "Your brother is amazing. He's so funny and cute. I'm so glad we met."

"How did you two meet? I don't think Nate ever told me," Natasha asked. She was almost afraid to hear the answer. She'd discovered most of the women Nate dated had been picked up at his bar, and, from what Mason told her, he used every ridiculous, cheesy, stupid line imaginable to do it.

"At the bar." Dottie shrugged.

Natasha forced herself not to spout something rude and sarcastic; instead, she plastered a smile on her face and nodded.

"My sorority sisters dragged me in there when I turned twenty-one for a drink," Dottie continued. "Nate gave me a free margarita; it was love at first drink." Dottie burst out laughing. "He is awful cute, though, isn't he? But why am I asking you? You're his sister!"

Natasha laughed politely and glanced toward the kitchen. Not only had they interrupted her and Mason's first kiss, now she had to listen to the sorority girl fawn over her brother.

"Can I ask you a question?" Dottie continued. "Does Nate ever talk about me?"

Oh, good lord, what is this? High school?

Natasha kept her thoughts to herself. She shook her head and willed her eyes not to roll back in her head. "No, not really."

"Oh." The dejected look on Dottie's face almost made Natasha feel sorry for her. Almost.

Natasha leaned over the end of the couch. "Hey! Hurry with those drinks, would you?" she yelled. "And make sure they're cold."

Nate peered around the corner. "Maybe you should relax, Tash."

Natasha stuck her tongue out at him as he returned to the living room with two bags of chips and a container of dip. He set everything on the table, perched on the arm of the couch next to his sister, and ruffled her hair.

"What's up, Nattie?"

Natasha rolled her eyes at Nate's use of her childhood nickname, crossed her arms over her chest, and rested her head against the back of the couch. "Not much. How are things with you, big brother?"

"Great." Nate poked her in the side. "Why do you ask?"

She looked pointedly at Dottie, who was digging through her purse and not paying attention to Natasha and Nate at all.

"What?" Nate mouthed.

Natasha shook her head. "Later," she mumbled.

Nate shrugged and sat down next to Dottie. He put his arm around her and kissed her neck, making her giggle.

Natasha sighed. It shouldn't bother her that Nate was having fun with the younger woman, at least until he found out Dottie was falling for him.

Mason stuck a glass of wine in Natasha's face and sat down beside her. He bumped his knee against hers and smiled.

Her stomach flip-flopped, and heat rushed through her. She couldn't wait to recreate that kiss later.

Chapter 13

Mason

Mason splashed cold water on the back of his neck. He squeezed his eyes shut and tried to think of stupid, mundane shit to take his mind off the feel of Natasha's body under his. It had been hours since it happened, but it was going to take a cold shower to turn off these feelings.

It didn't help that he'd spent two hours sitting inches away from her, inhaling the scent of her strawberry shampoo and listening to her throaty laughter. He'd tried to sleep, but he couldn't stop thinking about their kiss, which led to him thinking about other things they could have done before Nate interrupted them. It took all his self-control not to invite her into his bedroom at the end of the night, but they weren't there yet, despite how badly he wanted it.

Mason wasn't sure *where* they were actually. Natasha told him she had feelings for him, but it had ended there.

Were they dating? Were they not dating? He didn't know, and it drove him crazy.

He opened the bathroom door and tiptoed past a sleeping Natasha. Seeing her sprawled across the couch, with one leg hanging over the edge and the blankets kicked off, tempted Mason to wake her with a kiss and finish what they'd started. When he took a step toward the couch, Nate's door opened and his best friend came out, clad in just his boxers.

"Pants, dude," Mason whispered.

Nate jumped and swore quietly. "What are you doing out here? Ogling my sister?" He chuckled.

Mason scoffed. "No. It's not my fault she sleeps on the couch that I have to pass every time I go to the bathroom."

Nate put his hands up. "Okay, okay. I was only kidding. Sheesh."

"Why aren't you in there with Dottie?" Mason asked.

"Dottie left a couple of hours ago, and I needed a drink," Nate answered. "Not that it matters why I'm walking around my house in the middle of the night. You know, you look like you could use a drink, too."

"I need about a thousand of them," Mason muttered. "I'm going to bed." He spun around and stomped to his room. He wanted to slam the door, but he didn't want to wake up Natasha.

"Dammit," he muttered under his breath.

———

Mason had been on edge since he and Natasha kissed. He hadn't been able to get a second alone with her since then; Nate was always around when they were home. Neither of them had been home much, anyway; Natasha was working a lot to get ready for an upcoming show at the Lakeside Thespians Dinner Theatre, while he had been busy with several weddings and family photo shoots. They hadn't even set up Natasha's new headshots because of their conflicting schedules.

Any time they were together, the sexual tension between them tore him apart. He longed to take her into his arms and kiss her. Hell, he wanted more than that. He couldn't sleep, and his concentration was shot. He lived on coffee and energy drinks for the time being.

Their discussion about Natasha's feelings hadn't changed anything. Kissing her hadn't changed anything. She was still the unattainable woman torturing him with her presence.

Mason was determined to end his constant questions and the incessant wondering about where he stood with Natasha. He needed to suck it up and talk to her, tell her he reciprocated her feelings, and find out if they could try to make a relationship between the two of them work. If he was going to continue living in the same house with her, he had to know the truth.

"Earth to Mason!" A loud knock on the bar top pulled him out of the fugue he'd fallen into. He was so lost in his own head he forgot he was at the bar with a drink in front of him.

"What the hell is up with you, bro?" Nate asked. "You haven't been yourself for more than a week. You're all moody and contemplative."

"And you've been reading your word-of-the-day emails again, haven't you?"

Nate narrowed his eyes. "Stop trying to change the subject. What is going on with you?"

Mason took a deep breath. "I kissed Tasha," he blurted out.

Nate dropped the cloth he used to clean the bar on the floor and stared at Mason. "You what?"

"I kissed your sister," Mason repeated. He picked up his drink and downed it in two swallows. He coughed and winced as the alcohol burned his throat.

The grin on Nate's face almost split it in half. "It's about damn time."

"You know, most guys want their best friend to stay *away* from their sister," Mason said.

Nate laughed. "Most guys don't have you for a friend, either. You're a good guy, Mace. I'd be crazy not to want my sister with you."

"Would you feel the same way if you knew she has feelings for me?"

"She finally told you?" Nate asked.

"You knew?"

Nate snorted. "Of course I knew. She's my sister. Tasha talked to me, told me she liked you, and asked my advice. I told her to talk to you."

Mason sat up straighter, downed his drink, and glared at Nate. "Did you tell her how I feel about her?"

"No, I didn't. She needs to hear that shit from you, Mace, not me." He leaned on the bar and looked his friend in the eye. "Besides, I wouldn't do that to you. You and my sister need to work this out on your own. I'll be a sounding board, to both of you, but that's it. I am not playing middleman. We're not in high school anymore."

"If I recall correctly, you didn't help me in high school either," Mason pointed out.

Nate nodded. "You're right, I didn't. I didn't think you two should have gotten together back then. Tasha was still figuring out who and what she wanted to be. I think she would have broken your heart if you had dated in high school."

Mason narrowed his eyes. "You don't think she'll break it now?"

"I don't." Nate leaned on the bar. "My sister has spent a lot of time figuring out who she is. By the time we were in high school, she was sick of being 'Nate and Nattie.' Distancing herself from me—which meant distancing herself from you—gave her a chance to figure out who she was without me. Without us. She needed that. She learned a lot about herself, and she learned some hard lessons. I don't know if she's got it figured out yet, or if she knows who she is or what she wants. Tasha just has to figure out how to go after what she wants and get it."

"So maybe I won't be her brother's annoying best friend anymore?" Mason said.

"Eh, I don't know. She still might think you're annoying." Nate winked. "Wait, when you kissed her, she kissed you back, right?"

"Yes, she did. But we haven't really talked since it happened."

Nate rolled his eyes. "You need to talk to her."

Mason glared at Nate. "Don't you think I know that? I haven't had a chance. Life keeps getting in the way. *You* keep getting in the way. It's crowded in that tiny house; whoever said three is a crowd wasn't lying."

"Nah, three's company, bro. It's fun."

Mason threw a balled-up napkin at Nate's face and laughed. "I need to talk to her because I can't keep living in the same house with her, not knowing what's going on between us."

"Are you going to tell her how you feel?"

Mason nodded. "Yeah, I have to. She told me how she feels, so I owe it to her to be honest about my feelings for her."

"Thank God," Nate said. "And it only took eighteen years."

Mason grimaced. "Twenty. Thanks for reminding me how much time we wasted."

"It'll be fine. You'll see. I think everything will work out." Nate poured Mason another drink. "When are you gonna talk to her?"

Mason shrugged. "I don't know. I should probably wait until after her show opens. She's been so busy—"

"Hey, you know what?" Nate interrupted. "The theater is having their opening night party here at the bar. I'm giving them the back room for the night. You could come by the bar and talk to her then. If everything goes well with the show, she'll be in a good mood. It would be the perfect time to talk to her."

"That's a great idea." Mason rapped his knuckles on the bar. "I think that's what I'll do."

Nate's impossibly huge grin seemed to grow even wider. Mason shook his head and laughed. Who knew his best friend would encourage him to date his twin sister?

———

Mason spent the next week planning. He ordered flowers, planned to be off work from the hospital that night, and then convinced Natasha he wasn't going to be at her show because he had to work. He decided he wanted to surprise her instead, showing up at the party with flowers and sweeping her off her feet. At least, that was how he imagined it.

He prayed it worked.

Unfortunately, Natasha was angry with him for ditching her on opening night; their other friends, Summer and Gavin, and Oscar and Vera, planned on attending. Avery would be there as well. Nate couldn't make it because of staffing issues at the bar, and Mason had her convinced he wouldn't be there. Even though she hadn't come out and said it, it pissed her off he wasn't coming.

The day of the show, she asked Mason again if he would be there. He had just returned from work and she was at the kitchen table doing paperwork. When he reiterated for the tenth time that he couldn't attend because of work, she'd crossed her arms and glared at him. "First, my brother ditches me, and now you."

"Tash, I can't. It's summer, and the hospital is short-staffed. I'm on duty."

The way her face fell broke his heart, but he stuck to his guns. "I'm sorry. I know you're disappointed."

She gave him a weak smile and shrugged. "It's okay. I understand. At least Avery will be there." She rose to her feet.

"Tash, I swear I'll make it up to you," Mason pleaded.

Natasha shrugged and nodded, but she wouldn't meet his eyes. "I have to get ready." She disappeared into Nate's bedroom.

An hour later, Natasha emerged from her brother's bedroom in full makeup, with her auburn red hair loosely curled and pinned up so it framed her face. She had on a tight white tank top and short little shorts that emphasized her figure, fitting for the part of a cheerleader in the *Mean Girls* musical. Mason's breath caught in his throat, and he couldn't tear his eyes away from her.

"You look amazing," he said.

Natasha smiled, though it didn't reach her eyes. She didn't say anything as she gathered her things to take to the theater. Mason almost told her the truth just so he could see her smile.

He knew she was angry, and he hated to be deceptive, but when he showed up at the party later that night, he wanted her to be surprised.

She finished shoving everything in her backpack, grabbed her dress off the back of the bathroom door, and headed for the door.

"Good luck tonight!" Mason called after her.

Natasha froze with her hand on the doorknob. "Break a leg," she said. "You're supposed to say break a leg." She walked out without looking back.

———

Mason was on his way out of the door when his phone rang. He fully intended to decline the call, but when he saw it was Mr. Ward, his boss, he had to answer. Mr. Ward had been out of town for weeks—in Missoula with his grandchildren—so they had never discussed Mason buying the business; in fact, Mason thought he forgot.

So, instead of declining the call, he answered.

"Hello, Mr. Ward."

"Mason, how are you?"

"I'm doing well," Mason replied. "How's Missoula?"

"Wonderful." His boss cleared his throat. "How are things at the studio?"

"Busy as usual. Are you planning on coming back to Lakeside soon, sir?"

"That's why I'm calling," Harry explained. "I'm not coming back to Lakeside. The movers will clear out my house next week. I had my lawyer draw up papers to transfer the business to you."

Mason froze, unable to take another step. He wasn't sure he'd heard Harry correctly. "With all due respect, Mr. Ward, I appreciate the offer, but we haven't discussed price or anything like that. I'm not even sure I can afford to *buy* the business from you."

Harry chuckled. "My lawyer will deliver the paperwork to the studio on Wednesday. Look it over, and then we'll talk."

"Um ... okay. I'll ... I'll do that," Mason replied.

Once they'd said their goodbyes, Mason climbed in his truck and stared out the window. He could just see the lake through the cluster of houses, and his heart thumped in his chest. If this was for real, his life would change forever. Owning his own photography studio, even in tiny Lakeside, Montana, would be the dream come true.

He refused to get his hopes up, as he hadn't even seen the paperwork yet. More than likely, it would be out of his reach. Everything he'd ever wanted in life had been out of his reach. Why would this be any different?

Mason put the car in gear, but his enthusiasm for the surprise he'd planned was gone. Natasha was one of those things in his life that had always been out of reach, and nothing had changed. Chasing after her was an unattainable dream. He glanced at the bouquet on the passenger seat. A sense of dread crept over him—maybe this was a mistake.

He backed out of the driveway, but he second-guessed himself all the way to the theater. By the time he parked in the back of the lot, he had talked himself in and out of talking to Natasha about his feelings for her. When he stepped out of the truck, he still didn't know what he was going to do, but he squared his shoulders and went inside anyway.

Maybe I'll let fate decide.

Chapter 14

Natasha

The show was a phenomenal success, better than expected. A full house packed the theater, the crowd was into it, and the theater's owner was ecstatic. Natasha couldn't have been happier. The only thing that would have made it better was if Mason could have been there.

She regretted being angry with him; it wasn't his fault he had to work. Mason would have been there if he could have. As soon as she saw him, she planned to let him know she wasn't mad that he wasn't able to be at her show. Nothing could kill her good mood.

Once the final curtain fell, Natasha hurried to the dressing rooms to grab her stuff. She planned to duck out early so she could set up for the party.

Thanks to Nate, the opening night after-party was being held at the Time Out Bar and Grill. Natasha arrived first so she could get everything ready. Grateful for a minute alone, she took a second to duck into the bathroom. She smoothed the skirt of her forties-style, blood-red dress, checked her tightly curled hair, and carefully re-applied her makeup in the mirror. She'd spent a lot of time getting her look perfect, and the result pleased her.

She desperately hoped Mason would show up for the party. She sent him a text inviting him, hoping he would know it meant she wasn't angry anymore. He responded with a thumbs up, and nothing else. It wasn't a yes, but it also wasn't a no. She didn't even know what time he got off work.

It wasn't long before the cast and crew arrived, so Natasha shifted into hostess mode, greeting everyone and directing them to the back room of the bar. Once she had everyone settled and mingling, she went out front to thank her brother again for the use of the back room for the party. The crowded bar was no surprise; it was always busy. Nate worked his butt off to make this the most popular bar in Lakeside, and he succeeded. Natasha stepped behind the bar and tapped Nate on the shoulder.

When he turned around, she threw her arms around him and hugged him. "Hey, thanks for letting us use the bar for our after-party," she said.

"You're welcome," Nate replied. He kissed her on the cheek. "Anything for my sister, but I have some bad news. Trista is out sick, so I'm shorthanded. You're gonna have to help." He shoved a tray of drinks into her hands. "Take this back there, will you? And, if you need anything, I'll do my best to get it to you. I called another server to come in, but I haven't heard from her. We're swamped thanks to the pre-Labor Day crowd."

"I'll help with my party," she offered. "Almost everything is back there anyway—appetizers, food, bottled drinks—so we're good. I'll get any other drinks we need. Don't worry about anything." Natasha kissed Nate's cheek and headed for the back room with the tray balanced on one hand.

Fifty people packed the room, spread out across the remodeled back patio. Last summer, Nate remodeled the bar to make more room for indoor events. He'd had the back patio enclosed and turned into a sprawling room, with tables, chairs, a small bar in the corner, and a restroom. It was the perfect spot to host a party. Natasha set the drinks on the table, then she went to the sound system, plugged in her phone, and started the music. Before she knew it, people packed the dance floor, and the alcohol flowed. She made several trips back and forth to the front of the bar, keeping everything and everyone stocked with their favorite drinks. After a couple of trips, her friends volunteered to help, giving her the chance to hang out with everyone.

Just after eleven, Natasha saw Mason come through the door. She stood on her tiptoes and waved at him. His silver-gray eyes landed on her, and a grin spread across his face. He hurried across the room, wrapped an arm around her waist, and kissed her temple. He pulled his other hand out from behind his back and handed her a bouquet of a dozen pink carnations.

"My favorite!" She kissed him on the cheek. "Thank you! How did you know?"

"Seriously? I've known you for twenty years. What kind of friend would I be if I didn't know what your favorite flower is?" He hugged her close. "The show was magnificent. And you were fabulous."

"Wait? Were you there? I thought you had to work?"

Mason shrugged. "Please don't be mad, but I lied; I wanted to surprise you. I wouldn't leave you hanging like that."

Natasha hugged him tight, her cheek pressed to his chest, his heart pounding in her ear. "Thank you, Mace. I appreciate it more than you know. You are amazing."

Mason blushed and cleared his throat. "There was no way I could disappoint you. Hey, can I steal you away for a minute? I need to talk to you."

Natasha's stomach flipped. She nodded, so Mason took her hand and led her outside.

Should I be nervous?

Once outside, Natasha leaned against the porch railing and tried to act like her heart wasn't trying to pound its way out of her chest. She swallowed past the lump rising in her throat. "Okay, what's up?"

"I wanted to talk to you," Mason said. "About you and me."

She'd expected this, but that didn't quell her nerves. Even though she had told Mason about her growing feelings for him, and they had kissed, they hadn't really talked about what that meant, if it meant anything. They'd never talked about Mason's feelings.

Natasha took a deep breath and nodded. "It is probably time we talked, isn't it? There's a lot of air to clear."

Mason nodded. "I agree. We need to talk."

Natasha dropped into a chair on the patio and folded her hands in her lap. "So, you and me, huh? Are we ... are we a thing now?"

"You sound like you think that's a bad thing," Mason said.

Natasha shook her head. "No, I don't think it's a bad thing. I want to talk about us. We *need* to talk about us."

"Oh? Is this going to be more of the 'I have feelings for you, Mason' discussion, or are we going to figure out what we both want to do? I know what I want from you, Tasha. What about you? Do you know what you want?"

"I think I know what I want. I was just afraid to admit it. In fact, I fought it like crazy, but I don't want to fight it anymore." She stood up, stepped close to Mason, and put a hand on his chest, her finger circling the button on his shirt. She looked up into his mesmerizing gray eyes and smiled. "I like the thought of us together, Mason; I think it's a good thing."

Actually, she loved the thought of her and Mason together. She could picture them together for a long time, if not forever, but she wanted to take her time, make sure it would last. No rushing into it headlong or doing something stupid.

Her words brought a smile to his face. "Really?"

"Yes, really."

Mason slid an arm around her waist, brushed the hair from her face, and pulled her close. "You don't know how long I've waited to hear you say that." Mason rested his chin on the top of her head. "Are you sure about this? About us?"

Natasha nodded. "I am. I promise. But—"

Mason released her with a sigh. "There's always a but, isn't there?"

Natasha stood on her tiptoes and pressed a lingering kiss to his lips. She took his hand and squeezed it. "Hear me out. My breakup with Brick is still kind of fresh and honestly, sometimes it still hurts. I want to do this, but I want to take it one day at a time, see where it takes us. Are you okay with that?"

Mason nodded. "I've waited twenty years; I think I can wait a bit longer."

Natasha snorted. "Twenty years? No pressure though, right?"

"No pressure," Mason whispered.

"How about you kiss me to seal the deal?" Natasha asked.

Mason lifted her off her feet, his lips on hers. He kissed her until she couldn't breathe. Kissing Mason could easily become her new favorite thing. Reluctantly, she pulled away.

"We should go inside before people come looking for me."

Mason groaned and set her back down. "Fine. But you're going home with me tonight."

Natasha burst out laughing. "Okay, if you insist. I'll go home with you tonight." She kissed him again. "Come on, let's go inside."

———

The party was a tremendous success. Everyone ate, drank, and partied way too hard. As for Natasha, she had too much to drink. Her celebratory mood had as much to do with the success of the show as it did with her new relationship with Mason. For the first time in a long time, Natasha let loose.

By the end of the night, walking turned out to be a chore, as did staying upright. She leaned on Mason as they made their way up the sidewalk to their front door. He propped her against the wall while he unlocked the door, then he put his arm around her and helped her inside.

Once Mason set her on the couch, Natasha kicked off her shoes and stretched out. Mason got her a bottle of water and sat on the floor. Natasha ran her fingers through his long, black hair, twisting the strands around her fingers.

"I love your long hair," she murmured. "When you grew it out in high school—."

Mason rested his cheek on the couch next to her leg and smiled. "You told me you hated it."

"I lied." Natasha giggled. "I lied about a lot of stuff in high school. And maybe some things in college."

"Oh, really?" Mason raised an eyebrow. "What exactly did you lie about?"

Natasha closed her eyes and giggled again. "I lied when I told you Courtney Johnson didn't like you."

What am I doing? Too much alcohol, and I can't keep my mouth shut? she thought.

Mason chuckled. "Jealous?"

"Yes," Natasha whispered. "I didn't want you to date anybody. Nobody was good enough for you."

Natasha never told anyone about Courtney Johnson. Back in high school, Courtney had a crush on Mason. When she'd approached Natasha in math class to ask her about Mason, Natasha lied and told Courtney that Mason wasn't interested in dating anyone. She'd then told Mason that Courtney didn't like him. Natasha couldn't imagine the two of them together, so she made sure it didn't happen.

Mason stared at her, the intensity of his gaze boring into her soul. She took a sip of the water, but she couldn't swallow past the lump in her throat.

"Nobody was good enough for me?" Mason whispered.

Natasha considered lying, but she'd already gone too far. Might as well strive for honesty. "Not as far as I was concerned. The thought of you with anybody else always rubbed me the wrong way. I didn't think anybody would understand you like I did."

Mason turned to face her, his chin resting on the couch cushion. "You're the only woman in the world who has ever understood me." He cupped her face with his large hand, his thumb brushing her cheek. He kissed her, his lips soft against hers.

Natasha sighed and rested her head on his shoulder. "Take me to bed."

"I thought you wanted to take things slow?" Mason said.

"Maybe I changed my mind," she whispered.

Mason laughed. "Maybe you've had too much to drink."

She giggled again. "I had a lot of wine."

"And a couple of margaritas, and those five or six shots when you swore you could drink Ted under the table." Mason brushed her hair away from her face. "You need sleep."

"I need *you*," Natasha responded.

She wanted Mason, needed him. The desire was an ache in her soul she couldn't contain anymore.

Mason climbed to his feet, then he helped Natasha off the couch and led her to his bedroom. Her heart pounded in anticipation, sobering her up. He stood beside the bed as she stretched out across it and stared up at him, waiting. Instead of stripping off his clothes like she hoped, Mason grabbed the blanket from the end of the bed and pulled it up to her shoulder before lying down beside her. He brushed her hair off her face and kissed her forehead.

"Go to sleep, Tasha. We have all the time in the world."

Natasha sighed and closed her eyes. "All the time in the world," she whispered before she dozed off.

Chapter 15

Mason

Mason woke up alone. He was on one side of the bed while the other side was empty, the blanket thrown off and the pillow rumpled. He scrubbed a hand over his face, pushed a hand through his hair, and shoved himself to his feet. Mason opened the bedroom door and saw the living room was empty.

"Tasha?" he called.

Silence.

Great. I take her to bed and wake up alone the next morning. Did I already screw it up?

Nate's bedroom door opened, and he poked his head out. "She's not here; I don't think she came home last night. The couch was empty when I got home around three." He stepped into the living room, pulling his bedroom door closed behind him. "Did she talk to you?"

"She was here last night." Mason headed for the kitchen, Nate right on his heels.

"What do you mean 'she was here?'" A grin spread across Nate's face. "Wait a minute. Was she in your room?" The grin changed to a grimace. "Ew, don't answer that."

Mason didn't look at his best friend as he pulled the stuff for coffee from the cupboard. "She was in my room, but nothing happened. She had a lot to drink last night. I took her in there, covered her with a blanket, and we both went to sleep. Then I woke up alone."

Nate leaned against the counter and crossed his arms. "My sister slept in your bed last night. Does that mean what I think it means?"

"It means we're figuring things out," Mason said.

"Are you a couple or not?"

Mason nodded. "We're taking it slow, though, so don't make a big deal out of it, okay?"

"But it is a big deal. Isn't it?"

Mason laughed. "For me, yes. And I guess for her, too. She's still hurting from the breakup with Brick, so she doesn't want to rush into something new."

"Understandable." Nate clapped him on the back. "I'm glad to hear it, bro. I always thought you two were meant to be."

"Nate?" The woman's voice echoed through the house. "Where'd you go?"

Mason raised an eyebrow. "That didn't sound like Dottie," he whispered.

Nate shook his head. "It's not; Dottie and I broke up a couple of days ago. She was too young for me." He shrugged. "You know I'm not in any hurry to settle down. Dottie was getting too serious. Don't worry; I let her down easy."

"Nate!"

"Be right there," he yelled. He turned back to Mason. "About my sister—"

"Is this where you tell me if I hurt her, you'll kill me?" Mason asked.

"I think you already know that." Nate chuckled. "Seriously, though, she's my sister, and she's trusting you with her heart. Don't break it." He spun around and darted through the living room, back to his bedroom.

"No pressure," Mason muttered under his breath.

Once the coffee was done, he poured himself a cup and returned to his room. He didn't feel like meeting Nate's latest conquest, so he'd hide in his room and watch TV until she left. As he sat down on the bed, he glimpsed a piece of paper stuck between the pillows. It was a flyer that had probably been stuck on the front door, or maybe his car window. Scribbled on the back was a note from Natasha.

Mason-

> *Sorry I had to leave! I had to get down to the theater and take care of last night's box office receipts. I'll talk to you soon, I promise!*

Tash
P.S. Thank you for being a gentleman last night. You were right, of course. I was too drunk for us to do anything.

Mason smiled to himself. At least he hadn't screwed things up. He'd made the right decision last night, despite certain body parts insisting otherwise. It hadn't been easy to turn Natasha down, do the right thing, and be a gentleman. In fact, it had sucked, but he knew in the end, it was what had to happen. He was glad he'd listened to his head and not his groin, for he and Natasha had plenty of time to figure things out.

———

The large manila envelope sat in the center of the table, beckoning Mason to open it. He'd been sitting on the couch for almost an hour, staring at it, afraid to open it and shatter his dream of owning the photography studio.

He hadn't told anyone about the proposed deal between him and Harry Ward, fearing he'd jinx it if anyone else knew. But now that the papers were here, he regretted not talking to Nate about it. Despite his age, Nate was a shrewd businessman who'd grown a tiny bar with no customer base into a thriving business in less than five years. If anyone could give him sound business advice, it was his best friend.

As if on cue, the front door slammed. Nate tossed his keys on the kitchen table, grabbed a bottle of water from the fridge, and plopped on the couch next to Mason.

"What are you doing?" he asked. "I texted you like ten times, and you never answered. Tasha's meeting us at the bar in an hour."

Mason nodded at the envelope on the table.

Nate glanced at it, raising his eyebrows. "What is that?"

"It's a proposal from Mr. Ward. He wants to sell me the photography studio."

"What?" Nate scrambled to grab the bulky envelope but stopped. "Why didn't you tell me?" He glanced at Mason, hand poised and waiting for his friend's permission to rip it open. When Mason nodded, Nate tore open the envelope and dumped the papers out.

"You read it," Mason said. "Tell me what it says. How much is Harry asking?"

Nate was silent as he skimmed the paperwork, taking him too long read, as far as Mason was concerned. After several minutes, Mason punched him on the shoulder.

"What does it say? How much does he want?"

Nate laid the paperwork on the table. "Nothing."

"What? You're mistaken. Read it again."

"I read it more than once, bro. Harry doesn't want anything. All he wants is a legally binding agreement that you will keep the studio open in Lakeside for at least one year. After the year is up, you are welcome to sell it, close it, whatever you want to do. He said the best thing about owning the studio has been the reputation he has built in this town and the relationships he has established. He doesn't want to drop it like a hot potato when the business is flourishing."

Mason sagged against the back of the couch. The studio was his; all he had to do was keep it open for a year. Given that he had no plans to go anywhere, it couldn't have been a better deal.

"What do you think?" Mason asked.

"What do I think?" Nate said. "I think it's crazy. But I also know Harry. He's struggled since his wife passed away. He doesn't enjoy being away from his kids and grandkids, so this gives him a way out. If you didn't work for him, he'd close up shop and move. He probably wouldn't even bother selling it, just hang a closed sign in the window and walk away."

"So, should I do it?"

Nate nodded. "It's a once-in-a-lifetime opportunity. If you don't take advantage of it, you'd be stupid. Hell, if you don't do it, I might call Harry and tell him I'll take it off his hands. I think I know a photographer who could run it for me." Nate winked.

"Hilarious." Mason took a deep breath and slowly exhaled. "Where do I sign?"

———

"Where are we going?" Natasha asked.

"You'll see," Mason said.

Natasha made a face. "I don't like surprises, Mace. You know that."

"I'm not trying to surprise you, I swear. The place is off the beaten path. We have to walk."

"Am I going to get all hot and sweaty? If so, any photographs you take won't look so great."

"We won't have to walk far; it's not too far off the road." Mason turned down a dirt road two miles out of town and followed it for another mile. He parked in an enormous field and gestured for Natasha to get out of the truck.

Natasha jumped out of the truck, hiked her backpack higher on her shoulder, and dropped her sunglasses into place. "Which way?"

Mason pointed at a small hill two hundred yards away. "There's a small meadow that butts right up to the lake on the other side of that hill. The beach is gorgeous. It's a great place to get some nature shots for your portfolio. And mine. Come on."

"You better pray it's worth it," she grumbled. "I hate hiking."

Mason forgot Natasha didn't love the outdoors; she didn't like hiking, camping, or anything like that. None of that interested her, which always amused him since they lived in one of the most beautiful states in the union. He loved exploring, especially around Lakeside and Flathead Lake.

While hiking, Mason took Natasha's hand and helped her climb over a fallen tree and maneuver past some overgrown shrubs. He kept hold of her hand as they hiked toward the hill in the distance.

"It will be worth it, I promise," he said.

The two of them had been dating for a little over three weeks, and it had been the best three weeks of his life. Because they lived together, they were together constantly. Mason loved every minute. But, as Natasha requested, they were taking things slow, easing into a relationship twenty years in the making. As far as Mason was concerned, they could move at a snail's pace as long as Natasha belonged to him. He'd been patient for twenty years, so he could be patient a while longer until she was ready.

It took twenty minutes to reach the small beach and meadow. Mason grinned as Natasha froze in place, her mouth comically hanging open as she took in the lake's beauty. It was quiet here: no boats charging past, their wake sending waves on the shore, no people clamoring for a spot on the beach, no kids yelling, or college students catcalling. The sun reflected off the crystal-clear water, and the green of the trees appeared brighter and more vibrant.

Mason took everything in with a photographer's eye— the contrasting colors in the grass and leaves, the pink-and-purple flowers, and the blue sky. Natasha would look even more gorgeous than usual against the backdrop of the lake. He pulled out his camera and dropped his backpack to the ground. He quickly snapped a couple of pictures of Natasha, since she wasn't looking.

"Hey! I wasn't ready!" She made a face and flipped him off.

Mason snapped another photo before lowering the camera. "Those make the best shots."

Natasha trudged across the meadow and dropped her backpack beside his. She spun around, her back to him, and looked over her shoulder. Her eyes were hooded, the smile on her face demure yet alluring at the same time. It had his stomach dropping to his toes and his upper lip sweating. He took another picture before he grabbed her and kissed her.

"We aren't going to get many pictures taken if you stop to kiss me after every shot," she said when he released her.

Mason sighed. "I know. You just looked so irresistible, and now that I don't have to hold back—" He shrugged. "Besides, I enjoy kissing you."

"I enjoy kissing you, too," she whispered. "But before we get completely distracted, let's get the new headshots done. Then you can kiss me all you want."

Mason chuckled. "Sounds like a good plan."

They spent the next hour taking a multitude of photos. Mason couldn't get enough of Natasha—she was unbelievably photogenic. Of course, he was biased; he found her beautiful no matter what.

Once he finished photographing Natasha, he took a few minutes to walk along the edge of the lake with his camera in hand. Every inch of Flathead Lake, especially the area around Lakeside, was stunning; he could spend hours and hours taking photos of the area. In fact, he had spent hours doing just that, losing himself in the lake's beauty.

"Mason!"

He hurried back to Natasha. She must have had more in her backpack than the little bag of makeup he'd seen her take out earlier, because when he got back to her, he found her sitting on a large blanket with sandwiches, two small bags of carrots, and juice boxes spread out in front of her.

"What's this?" he asked.

Natasha grinned and held up a sandwich. "Peanut butter-and-jelly."

Mason couldn't hold back the laughter. "My favorite! Thank God it's not bologna." He tucked his camera into his backpack, sat down beside her, plucked the sandwich out of her hand, and took a huge bite.

"This is delicious," he mumbled around a mouthful of food.

He devoured everything Natasha handed him, then stretched out on the blanket, with his hands clasped behind his head and his eyes closed. After a few minutes, Natasha laid down next to him, her head on his arm.

"What are you thinking about?" she asked.

"That this weather won't last much longer," Mason replied. "Now that Labor Day is over, the cold weather will head our way."

"That's what you're thinking about?" She giggled. "How romantic."

Mason chuckled. "Sorry. I'm not so great with the romance stuff, but I'll work on it."

"You could start by kissing me," she whispered.

He turned to face her, their knees touching. Mason dug his fingers into her hip, took her chin in his hand, and tipped her head back so he could stare into her eyes. He slid his hand up her side and into her hair, pulled her close, and kissed the corner of her mouth.

"Is that all you got?" Natasha asked, her breath warm against his skin.

Mason wrapped an arm around her back, the tips of his fingers brushing the skin between the waistband of her shorts and her t-shirt. He swiped his tongue across her bottom lip. Natasha opened her mouth, and his tongue brushed against hers. She opened her mouth more, allowing him to fully explore hers. His tongue moved over her teeth and lips, his nose brushing against hers as the kiss deepened. Natasha pulled out the rubber band holding his hair away from his face, twisted her fingers in his hair, and tugged slightly to pull him closer to her.

A tiny groan from Natasha sent a spark shooting through him, settling deep in his gut and causing an ache inside him he couldn't ignore. He rolled Natasha to her back, his knee between her legs, the kiss becoming something more, something stronger, something he didn't think either of them could fight.

Natasha wrapped herself around him, arms and legs, until he could barely tell where she ended and he began. He lost himself in the kiss, the world around him fading to a blur of colors and sounds that meant nothing as long as he was in her arms.

This was what he had wanted all his life, what he needed all of his life. She was his; she had always been his, she would always be his. Mason would do whatever it took to keep this woman by his side.

Chapter 16

Natasha

Natasha moaned and sank into the blanket as Mason's weight settled over her. This felt *right*, like it was meant to be, like it was the only thing in the world she had ever wanted or needed.

She closed her eyes and let herself go, let herself forget about everything and everyone. There was just Mason.

As the kiss deepened, Natasha's fingers itched to touch Mason's bare skin, to feel his tanned, taut body naked against hers. They'd been dating for three weeks, and Mason had been a perfect gentleman at her request. His touch ignited something in her, something that only he could satisfy. Natasha needed it, and she didn't want to wait any longer. The temptation was too great.

She shoved the unbuttoned flannel he wore off his shoulders and tugged it down his arms, tossing it aside. Mason's eyes widened, and a low grunt left him as Natasha traced the muscles in his back through the thin gray t-shirt he wore.

"I thought we were waiting," he whispered.

"I don't want to wait anymore, Mace. I want you. All of you."

Mason smirked. "Does that mean what I think it means?"

Natasha poked him in the shoulder. "Yes, you ass. Are you gonna make me say it?"

Mason nodded.

"Fine." Natasha twisted her fingers in Mason's hair and pulled, dragging him close so she could press her mouth against his ear. "I want you to make love to me, Mason."

Mason growled deep in the back of his throat, an animalistic sound that made her ache inside. Mason slipped his hand under the edge of her shirt and pushed it up her stomach, stopping halfway, his fingers dancing over her stomach that were not quite tickling, but sending delightful pings of desire traipsing through her. Natasha moaned, and Mason pulled the shirt all the way off, leaving her in just her bra.

Goosebumps rose on her skin as Mason's hands caressed her waist, goosebumps that had nothing to do with the cool air. A shiver danced along her spine. Natasha wrapped a leg around the back of Mason's thigh, slid her hand under his t-shirt, and coaxed him out of it.

Natasha kept her fingers tangled in Mason's hair, using them to hold him close as his mouth was on hers. They kissed, their bodies intertwined together, as his feverish body heated her from the inside out. When she moaned, Mason moaned in response. When she moved, Mason moved with her, their connection never breaking.

Mason moved to her neck, nipping at her skin and licking over the new love bites that marked her skin. His lips roamed over her body, over her breasts, down her stomach, and across her hips as he unbuttoned her shorts and slid them down her legs. Natasha kicked off her shoe, giggling when one shot up into the air and landed two feet from her head.

Mason chuckled and rose to his knees. "Let's try not to knock anybody out. What do you say?"

Natasha nodded and silently watched him remove her other shoe and her socks, then he pulled her shorts off and dropped them on top of her shoes. He caressed her leg for a moment before leaning down to kiss a trail up her legs, stopping to knead, lick, and suck her inner thighs.

This was a side of Mason she hadn't known existed. Sure, she had fantasized about him occasionally; after all, she was only human, but she never imagined those fantasies would come to fruition. She never imagined timid, good-guy Mason would be a bold, take-charge kind of lover.

When he bit her inner thigh, so close to where she desperately wanted him, Natasha threw her head back and thrust her hips forward, chasing Mason's sinful mouth. She wanted his mouth on her, needed to feel him devouring her, feasting on her.

Mason grabbed her hands and held them at her sides as he worked his way up her nearly naked body—kissing her stomach, licking her breasts, his tongue dancing over the lace covering her nipples. He nipped and sucked at the sensitive skin of her neck before he caught her lips in his and pushed his tongue into her mouth.

"Mason," she gasped when he eventually pulled away. "Jesus, I never imagined."

Natasha trembled, her body slick with sweat, and her breath tearing in and out of her throat. She dug her fingers into his hips, desperate to keep him close.

Mason slid his hands up her back, unhooked her bra, and added it to the growing pile of clothes.

"God, Tash, you're so beautiful," Mason murmured. "I want you so bad."

Natasha nodded and tugged on his hair. "I want you, too."

Mason took her breast in his mouth and, to her surprise, sucking not so gently. The shock of the pain mixed with pleasure made her hiss and arch her back, her hands fisting in the blanket beneath her. She'd never felt like this, never been this turned on by anyone, ever.

Mason released her and scrambled to his feet. He fumbled for his wallet, pulled a condom out, and stuck it between his lips. He yanked off his shorts and tossed them aside before dropping to his knees in front of Natasha. He dragged her lacy pink panties down her legs and threw them over his shoulder. He tossed the condom on the blanket next to her head, licked his lips, and stretched out, hovering over her. Then she couldn't see his face anymore because it was between her legs, his tongue and two fingers deep in her pussy. She screamed, the pleasure overwhelming her. There was no way she could hold back; gasps and moans escaped her as her body spasmed. Natasha let herself go, let herself get lost in the intensity of the feelings racing through her, with every muscle tightening as she came into Mason's mouth.

He held her, lapping at her wet center, his finger brushing over her swollen bud until she collapsed in a boneless, out-of-breath mess. When she could somewhat breathe again, Mason grabbed the condom, ripped it open, and slid it down his length. He pulled her legs around his waist and eased into her, eyes closed, not moving.

Natasha put her hand on his chest. "Don't stop, Mace. I want this. I want *you*."

That must have been all he needed. Mason gripped her hips, hard, his fingers digging into the flesh, and he slammed into her repeatedly. He whispered how beautiful she was, how much he wanted her, needed her.

Tangled together with bodies moving, hips thrusting, lips crashing together, and their breath mingling, the insane pleasure coursed through them as they raced toward their finish. Her name rumbled from Mason's chest as he came, his head thrown back and his long, black hair ruffled by the wind. Natasha dug her nails into his thighs as she writhed beneath him, her walls clenching around him and milking his cock dry.

Mason collapsed on top of her, his weight shifted to one side so he didn't crush her. He sighed and closed his eyes.

Natasha turned to face him, tracing his jawline with the tip of her finger. "That was amazing," she whispered. "I'm not sure it's ever been like that with anyone." She kissed his cheek. "Thank you."

Mason wrapped an arm around her and pressed a kiss to her temple. "You should always be treated like that. Worshipped, treasured."

"Sometimes I can't believe you're real." She giggled. "You're too good to be true."

A breeze blew through the meadow, whistling through the trees. Mason sat up and pushed a hand through his hair. "It's getting cold," he muttered.

The air had chilled, and the sun was low over the lake. As soon as she sat up, the cool air hit her flushed, hot skin, sending a shiver racing down her spine. She trembled and wrapped her arms around herself. Every year, she forgot how quickly the weather turned in Montana: warm during the day and cold at night.

"We should get back before it gets too dark," Mason said.

Natasha nodded, grabbed her clothes, and pulled them on. Mason did the same, rushing to cover himself as the wind picked up.

Once he was dressed, he climbed to his feet and held out his hand. "Come on."

Natasha took it and let him help her up. He pulled her into his arms and held her tight. She pressed her face against his chest and hugged him back.

They separated and quickly cleaned up their things, shoving everything into the backpacks. Mason held her hand as they hiked back through the woods to his truck parked alongside the road. He opened the door for her, helped her inside, and kissed her cheek before jogging around the front of the truck to the driver's side. He held her hand as they drove back to their place.

Natasha rested her head against the seat and closed her eyes. The hum of the tires on the road, Mason's warm hand wrapped around hers, and the dark night lulled her to sleep. For the first time in a long time, she was at peace.

———

The peace didn't last long. Their driveway was full of cars when they pulled in; it looked like they parked half the town in front of their house. Mason had to park three houses away.

Natasha jumped out of the truck and was immediately hit by the sound of loud, bass-filled music filling the night sky, pulling all the energy in the neighborhood toward their small house. Every light was lit, and the doors were wide open. People spilled into the yard.

"What the hell is this?" she yelled.

Mason shook his head. "Who the hell knows? Maybe Nate got bored?"

Natasha felt bad for their neighbors, forced to endure whatever was happening at their house. As they passed, Natasha saw their shy, introverted neighbor peering out her window with an irritated look on her face.

Mason took Natasha's hand as they made their way through the people clustered around the front door. As soon as they were inside, Mason called for Nate, but it was unlikely Nate had heard anything over the music. Mason must have spotted Nate, because he tightened his grip on Natasha's hand and dragged her through the crowd and into the living room. Nate stood in front of the TV with Oscar and Gavin.

"Mace! Tasha! You're finally home! Where the hell have you two been?" Nate said.

"Out," Mason grumbled. He swirled his finger in a circle. "What is all this?"

Nate made a face. "It's a party."

Mason sighed. Natasha squeezed his hand and smiled at her brother. "We know it's a party," she said, summoning every ounce of patience she had. "The question is, why is it here and not at the bar?"

"Oh, well, it started at the bar," Nate explained, "but then it kind of followed me home." He shrugged. "Who am I to say no?"

Natasha shook her head. "Are you ever going to grow up?" she asked.

Nate leaned over her, a huge grin on his face. "Nope."

Mason rolled his eyes and ducked into his bedroom. Natasha followed him.

"Hey, are you okay?" she asked.

"Yeah," Mason replied. "Nate drives me crazy sometimes. I wasn't expecting to come home to a party. I thought maybe we could hang out and watch movies or something."

Natasha stepped into his arms and rested her head on his chest. "I had a great time today. Don't let Nate and his partying attitude ruin it; we might as well go out there and join the madness."

Mason laughed and kissed the top of her head. "You're right. I'm being stupid. Let's go join the party."

Natasha linked her arm through Mason's and let him lead her back out to the party. Her mom always said to make the most of an unpleasant situation. While the party might not be bad, it wasn't ideal. They might as well have fun.

As soon as they emerged from the bedroom, the teasing began. When she kissed Mason on the cheek, Oscar yelled, "Get a room!" And when she glanced at Mason over her shoulder, Gavin started making kissing sounds, his eyes wide, and a delighted smirk on his face.

I think I need a drink.

Natasha excused herself to go to the kitchen to make margaritas. Being teased was no fun; if it continued, she needed a drink. Or two. Nate followed her and leaned against the counter beside her with a huge, cheesy grin on his face.

Natasha dropped the bottle of margarita mix on the counter and yanked open the freezer. She refused to look at her brother. "What is it you find so amusing, Nate?" she asked, with her head in the fridge.

Out of the corner of her eye, she saw her brother shrug. "Oh, you know. My best friend and my sister, that's all."

She shook her head; Nate's amusement astonished her. "Isn't it supposed to bother you I'm dating Mason? I thought brothers *didn't* want their sisters dating their best friends?"

Nate snorted. "Are you kidding? I've been waiting *years* for this moment."

Natasha jerked her head in his direction, margarita mix splashing onto the counter as she turned to stare at her brother. "What do you mean, *years*?"

"You know. Years. No pressure or anything, but you are the woman Mason has been waiting for his whole life. There isn't anything on earth that man loves more than you. No one, and I mean no one, can hold a candle to you. He has been in love with you since we were kids." Nate grabbed a chip out of the bowl on the counter and shoved it in his mouth, chewing loudly with his mouth open.

Natasha took a deep breath. *Years.* She pushed a hand through her hair. Nate had to be joking. There was no way Mason had been in love with her since they were children. *Love.*

Jesus, that was another thing. Was Mason really in love with her? And if he was, why hadn't he ever said anything to her? Her head spun.

"So, what you're telling me is that Mason has—" She couldn't finish the thought.

Apparently, Nate could. "—has been in love with you for most of his life," Nate said.

Natasha could only stare at her brother, unsure how to deal with this information. While she'd known Mason liked her, had in fact liked her for a while, she didn't know he'd been in love with her for years. Or that he saw her as some kind of "ideal" woman. That was a lot of pressure.

She spun the top off the tequila bottle and took a huge gulp. It burned and made her eyes water, but she didn't care.

Nate stared at her, mouth agape. "What the hell, Tash?"

"I need a drink," she snapped.

Nate plucked the bottle from her hand. "I don't think you need it straight from the bottle. What is wrong with you?"

"Nothing," she snapped.

Her brother raised an eyebrow, glanced over his shoulder at the people in the living room, and then took a step closer to his sister while lowering his voice.

"Are you okay?" he asked.

Natasha snorted. "Of course, I'm okay."

Nate narrowed his eyes and crossed his arms over his chest. "Don't you think I know when you're lying? Talk to me. What's wrong?"

Natasha pinched the bridge of her nose. "I guess I didn't realize Mason has had feelings for me for ... for a while. I always thought I was nothing more to him than your dumb twin sister."

Nate laughed and shook his head. "Sometimes you are so *thick*, Tash. Mason has loved you since we were six years old. How have you not seen it? How have you not realized that, for Mason, you are the only woman in the world? The perfect woman in one tiny, fiery, redheaded package."

"That's not fair," she whispered. "How am I supposed to live up to that?"

"No one is asking you to live up to anything," Nate said. "You and Mason are together; that's all that should matter."

"You don't get it, Nate." Natasha pushed a hand through her hair. "I have always had to live up to other people's expectations. Mom and Dad expected me to be like you: smart, business-savvy, and focused. They expected me to find a nice guy, settle down, run a business. I disappointed them when I decided to be an actress—"

"That's not true."

Natasha held up her hand. "Let me finish. I have spent my whole life trying to do what everyone expects me to do. Being what someone else wants or needs. I did it for our parents during high school. I did it for Brick after we started dating; hell, I did it for every guy I *ever* dated. And now, I have to do it again with Mason. It's not fair; it's not what I want."

"I don't think Mason expects anything of you," Nate said.

"You know what? I need to talk to Mason." She straightened her shoulders and gave her brother her best smile. "Could you please tell your best friend I'd like to speak to him for a minute?"

"Tasha—"

She pursed her lips and promised herself she wouldn't swear at her brother. "Please, Nate. Could you get Mason? I *need* to talk to him."

Nate nodded and did as she asked. At least some things were simple.

Hopefully, it's that easy with Mason.

Chapter 17

Mason

Nate came out of the kitchen like someone had lit a fire under his ass. He headed directly for Mason, grabbed his friend's arm, and pulled him away from the group surrounding him.

"You need to go talk to Tasha. Now," Nate said, his voice low so only Mason could hear him.

Mason glared at his friend. "What did you say to her?"

"Nothing." Nate shrugged. "Well, something, but I didn't think it was a big deal. Something about you being in love with her for years and that she has always been your ideal woman. I don't know. I think she's panicking."

Mason swore under his breath. "Jesus, Nate, you told her I've been in love with her for *years*? We've been dating for three weeks. I better talk to her." He pushed past Nate and made his way to the kitchen, elbowing people out of his way.

Natasha was in the corner of the kitchen, arms crossed over her chest and gnawing on her lower lip. Mason had barely set foot in the kitchen before she leaped across the floor and got in his face.

"Have you really been in love with me your entire life?" she asked.

The unmitigated anger in her voice caught him off guard. "Wh-what?" he stammered.

Natasha took a step back. "I asked if you have really been in love with me your whole life. According to Nate, you've loved me since you were six."

Mason nodded, nothing more than a tip of his chin, but it was more than enough to tell Natasha that yes, he had loved her since he was six. Her face fell, and it ripped his heart in two. He took a step toward her, but she put her hand up and stumbled back, her ass hitting the counter.

Natasha nodded. "Okay. That's, uh, wow. That's a lot to deal with. When you said you waited twenty years for me, I thought you were joking. Good lord, Mason. Twenty years?"

"Let me explain," Mason said.

"Can I ask you a question?" she blurted out before he could say anything else.

"Of course you can," he said.

"Do you even love *me*, Mace? Or do you love the *idea* of me?"

Mason's stomach flipped, and bile rose in the back of his throat. "I don't know what you mean."

Natasha took a step closer, her shoulders back, chin raised. "Sure you do. Do you love *me,* or do you love some version of me you've created in your head? The unattainable woman, your best friend's sister, the girl engaged to another man: is that who you love? That woman? Or me?" She stabbed a finger into her chest.

"You, Tasha," Mason replied. "I love *you*. I have loved you for a long time."

Natasha snorted and shook her head. "How can you be so sure? I don't think you even know the real me."

Mason froze, his fists clenched at his sides as a flicker of irritation sparked through him. If anybody knew Natasha Garin, it was him. He took a deep breath and paused before he spoke. "That's funny, Tash. Because I don't think you know the real you."

"What did you say?"

"You heard me," Mason said. "For years I've watched you try to fit the girlfriend mold of whoever you're dating. You acted however they wanted you to act. I never saw you be *you*. It makes me sick to think about you spending the last two years burying the real you so you could stay with a guy who never loved you or appreciated you. Shit, not just the last two years. You've wasted years chasing after something, sorry, *someone* to make you whole."

The light in her eyes dulled. "At least I didn't spend most of my life afraid to tell the woman I love how I feel."

Mason balked and flinched. "That's not fair," he whispered. "I waited for you. While you worked your way through Reggie, and Dave, and Mike, and Bobby, they broke your heart. I waited while Brick tore it to pieces. I gave you space. You had a chance to figure it out. I waited until you were ready. I waited until you knew who and what you wanted. I waited for you to figure out I was Mr. Right."

Natasha scrubbed a hand over her face. "You know what? Maybe I don't know what I want. Or who I want.

Maybe you aren't Mr. Right, Mason. Maybe you're just *Mr. Right Now*." She spun on her heel, ripped open the closet to snatch out her jacket and backpack, and was gone, out the front door and rushing past everyone.

The silence was deafening. All conversation had stopped; even the music wasn't playing. Mason didn't want to turn around; he didn't want to see the sad, pity-filled looks on the faces of his friends. Instead, he dug his keys out of his pocket and walked out the front door.

——

Mason drove around the block several times, but he didn't see Natasha anywhere. She couldn't have gotten far, not on foot. Lakeside was a small town; there weren't a lot of places she could go.

He pulled off the road and parked in the lot of the local grocery store. He grabbed his phone and quickly typed out a text to Natasha. He stared at it for several minutes before he deleted it and tried again.

[Mason: I'm sorry.]

He waited; his heart pounded when the three little bubbles appeared. After a few seconds, they disappeared. Five minutes went by, but Natasha didn't respond. He tossed his phone on the passenger seat. She needed time to cool off.

Mason closed his eyes and rested his head against the back of the seat. He screwed up, and he knew it. With Natasha and his feelings for her, he didn't always think straight; it had been like that for years. He reacted with emotion rather than thinking before he opened his mouth and inserted his foot.

Natasha's words repeated over and over in his head.

At least I didn't spend most of my life afraid to tell the woman I love how I feel.

She was right, to an extent. He had spent years afraid to tell Natasha how he felt about her. Mason had convinced himself that she wouldn't want him because he *was* Mason, her brother's best friend. Her friend. And definitely not her type. During high school, Natasha had gone for the big, strong, alpha male types: guys who played sports and ruled the school. That wasn't Mason. He didn't hit his growth spurt until the summer before senior year. He left to spend a month with his father and his new wife, returning to Great Falls six inches taller and sixty pounds heavier thanks to the growth spurt.

For the first time, girls paid attention to him, but not the girl he wanted. He could have done a circus act in front of Natasha, and she would still ignore him. She wanted anyone but Mason, regardless of what Mason or Nate thought.

Not that Natasha cared what they thought or bothered to hang around long enough to find out. She fell off the radar, avoiding her brother and Mason as if they had the plague.

Mason probably saw her three or four times over the next year. He knew Brick proposed, thanks to Nate, but that was the extent of his knowledge of Natasha's life.

However, the torch he carried for Natasha never extinguished. She was always there, always on his mind. But he kept his distance, waiting for things to change.

Then she'd stumbled through their door, and his entire world imploded.

Mason scrubbed a hand over his face. There was no use sitting here rehashing the past, the mistakes he'd made, and the opportunities he'd let get away. He put the truck in gear and turned it toward home.

———

The party was over by the time he got back to the house. The only cars in the driveway were Nate's and Natasha's. It gave him a glimmer of hope that she had come home.

Nate was in the living room, trash bag in hand, picking up empty cans and bottles. He glanced over his shoulder when Mason shut the front door, but he returned to cleaning when he saw who it was.

"She's not here," Nate said.

"Have you heard from her?" Mason asked.

Nate nodded. "She texted me. She went to Avery's. She wants to be left alone. Said she needs some time to think."

Mason leaned against the wall, crossed his arms, and shook his head. "I fucked up."

"You both fucked up." Nate tied off the bag, looked around the room at the remaining mess, grimaced, and pulled another bag out from under the sink. "My sister is a strong woman. It took her a while to figure it out and even longer to get out of that goddamn relationship with Brick, but she did. She's spent most of her life trying to be what everyone else wants: our parents, one boyfriend after another. Now that she's finally figuring out who she is and what she wants, it scares her to think she might have to conform to *your* idea of the perfect woman."

"I didn't ask her to do that," Mason interjected.

"No, you didn't. And that's her fuck-up. She assumed you wanted to change her, mold her into something she wasn't. You need to talk to her. She needs to talk to you. You two can figure this out. I know you can, if you talk it out."

"I know that," Mason said. "Does she?"

"She will." Nate sat on the couch, holding the bag between his knees. "I feel kind of responsible for this."

Mason crossed the room and sat beside his best friend. "Why? You didn't do anything."

"Oh, but I did." Nate sighed. "I like the idea of the two of you together. A lot. I've been pushing it. I wasn't helping either of you, but I was encouraging the relationship. Maybe I should have played the middleman and done my best to mediate your relationship. I think my input might have been helpful."

Mason snorted. "That's weird." He could only imagine the level of uncomfortable those kinds of conversations could have reached.

Nate burst out laughing. He dropped the trash bag on the floor and fell back against the couch, his hands over his face. "Oh, Jesus! What did I just say? Can you imagine?"

Mason chuckled. "Um, I'm trying not to."

Nate patted Mason on the shoulder. "Look, it will all work out. Tash needs some time to process shit, that's all. Give her some space."

"I've been giving her space for years, Nate. Maybe I'm sick of waiting."

Nate raised an eyebrow and stared at his best friend. "Are you serious? After all this time, after everything you've gone through, after finally getting the girl, now you're going to say you're done. Just like that?"

"No, it's not 'just like that.' I've been waiting for your sister since I was six. I waited through idiot boyfriend after idiot boyfriend, and I waited until I was the man she wanted. Or at least the man I thought she wanted. Problem is, I'm not sure I am the man she wants. Maybe I really am just Mr. Right Now. The rebound boyfriend, not the guy she's supposed to end up with."

"Do you really think she's using you as a rebound thing after Brick? Have some fun with an old friend, then move on to something better or improved?"

Mason shrugged. "I don't know anything anymore." He shoved himself to his feet. "I'm tired. I'm going to bed. We can talk about this more tomorrow when I can think straight."

"Mace, wait."

Mason ignored Nate, went into his room, and quietly closed the door. He fell into his bed, fully clothed and shoes on. He was suddenly exhausted and wanted to sleep for a week.

———

"So, she's still at Avery's?" Mason asked.

"Yeah," Nate answered. He tossed his keys on the kitchen table and sat down across from his best friend.

Mason groaned and dropped his head to the table, banging it on the flimsy wood. "How am I supposed to fix this?" he mumbled.

"I don't know if it's up to you to fix it, Mace. I think this one is on Tasha."

Mason rubbed a hand over his face, wincing at the rough stubble under his hand. "What is that supposed to mean?"

"My sister created this mess. She's got you wrapped around her little finger, and she knows it. She's known it for years. I think she took advantage of your feelings for her and, dare I say it, I think she might have used those feelings to her advantage."

Mason's head came up off the table, and he glared at Nate. "That's a pretty shitty thing to say about your sister."

Nate sighed and shook his head. "I know. Trust me, I feel like shit saying it." He cleared his throat. "Are you sure she didn't know you were in love with her? You never told her after you guys started this dating thing?"

"No, I didn't tell her," Mason muttered. "It's not really the best way to start a relationship. 'Hey Tasha, I've been in love with you for roughly twenty years. No pressure though.'"

"If you had just told her—"

Mason groaned. "Don't start that crap again."

Nate smacked his hand on the table. "I am gonna start this crap again." He leaned over the table, face drawn tight, brow furrowed, fists clenched. "You've been sitting on your ass for far too long. You could have told her in high school or college, or any time in between."

"There was always someone else, Nate. Your sister bounced from guy to guy throughout high school and college. Every time she broke up with one, I was there, picking up the pieces, being the friend she needed. Then she'd brush me off and move onto the next guy, leaving me in the dust, again." Mason shot to his feet, irritation fueling his need to move. "I dated Allison because I was tired of waiting for Tasha."

"Yeah, we both know how well that went," Nate snapped. "It lasted what, ten, eleven months before she realized you were head over heels in love with another woman? And while you were with Allison, trying to get over my sister, Tasha ended up with Brick, the world's biggest asshole."

Mason swung around, his finger in Nate's face. "That was not my fault."

Nate planted his hands on the table and stared at Mason. "No, you're right. It wasn't your fault. But maybe you could have stopped it. Jesus, you keep blowing it with my sister, and it pisses me off. If ever there were two people in this world who belonged together, it's you two."

"Don't you think I know that?" Mason asked. "But I'm not the only one who blew it. Instead of falling for the guy standing right in front of her, the guy who stood up for her, gave her a shoulder to cry on, and supported her when she needed it, she kept hooking up with idiots who walked all over her and broke her heart. We both screwed up."

"I just hope you two can fix it. Because that's my sister, Mason, and as much as I care about you, if push comes to shove, I'll pick her over you every single time. It would be a shitty choice, a damn near impossible choice, but one I'll make if I have to. And it will be my sister."

Struck speechless at Nate's declaration, Mason swung around and stalked away, angry tears clouding his vision. He was almost to his room when he hit the corner of the coffee table with his bare foot.

"God dammit!" he yelped. The pain radiated up his leg, forcing him to hop a couple of feet on one foot. His fist connected with the wall beside his bedroom door, as all his anger and frustration boiled to the surface and exploded in a rain of drywall dust and paint chips.

Chapter 18

Natasha

"Go away, Avery," Natasha mumbled. She shoved her head under the pillow and pulled the blankets up to her chin. She didn't want to talk to her friend, her brother, to anybody.

"I'm just leaving you some water and a couple of ibuprofens," Avery whispered. "I have a feeling you're going to need it."

Natasha half-expected Avery to say something more, to lecture her, or maybe agree with her, something, but she heard the door to the spare bedroom click closed. She waited until she was sure Avery wasn't lurking outside the door, ready to burst back in and talk, before she pushed the pillow to the floor and struggled to sit up. The stupid blankets twisted around her stupid legs, and the fight to untangle herself had her in tears. She swiped at her eyes with the corner of the bedsheet, grabbed the water and pills, then downed them in two swallows.

She leaned against the headboard, eyes squeezed shut as she prayed not to vomit. This was by far the worst hangover she'd had since college. Unfortunately, this hangover didn't come with memory loss; she remembered every detail of the previous day, from the photo shoot to the lovemaking, ending with the colossal fight witnessed by five or six dozen of Nate's closest friends.

Just thinking about the fight made heat rush to her cheeks and her heart race. It mortified her they'd fought in front of all those people, and that she'd said the things she said and Mason had said the things he'd said. Maybe she would stay in this room forever, then she wouldn't have to show her face to her friends ever again.

Not only was Natasha embarrassed, but she was pissed and hurt, too. Mason intentionally hurt her feelings, saying things he knew would rip her apart and destroy her. The man was intimately connected to her life, knew everything about her, even her dirtiest secrets, her heartbreaks and pain, and he'd thrown it in her face to hurt her.

Of course, she was no angel. She'd done the same to him, mocking him for not telling her how he felt about her all these years. She'd wanted to hurt him, to make him feel like she felt.

What were they doing? Why were they purposefully trying to hurt each other, lashing out, intent on causing pain? They were friends.

Or were they?

They'd crossed the line friends shouldn't cross; once that line was crossed, there was no going back. Natasha had known that going in, and so had Mason. Their fight the previous night meant the end of not only their so-called relationship, but the end of a twenty-year friendship.

The thought terrorized her and caused an ache deep in her soul, an ache she didn't think would easily heal.

"Oh, god," Natasha moaned, as realization hit her. She rolled to her side and pulled the blankets tight around herself. There was only one reason the end of her friendship with Mason could hurt so badly.

"Am I in love with Mason?" she whispered to herself.

—

Avery left her alone for the rest of the day, sneaking in to leave a sandwich around noon and again with a cup of tea about three. Natasha mumbled thank you both times, but she didn't move.

Her phone went off intermittently, but she didn't bother looking at it. Not now; maybe later, if her mood improved.

Around five, Natasha dragged herself out of bed and made her way down the hall to the bathroom. She could hear the TV playing downstairs and the quiet, murmured voices of Avery and Jacob. For a split second, she considered going downstairs, but she quickly changed her mind. She wasn't sure she could handle hanging out with the happy couple or the inevitable questions that might arise.

When she'd called Avery, after storming out of Nate and Mason's house, she'd kept her explanation to a bare minimum. The less said, the better. Somehow, Avery knew, and she didn't pry. She was a good friend.

Once she'd used the bathroom and washed her face, she returned to the bedroom. Natasha sipped the lukewarm tea and gnawed on the peanut butter-and-jelly sandwich as she checked her phone.

She had missed calls from Nate, Summer, and even her mother. There were two from Mason, and they had both come late last night. Had he really given up so quickly?

Natasha hit the button, held the phone to her ear, and waited. It only rang twice before he answered.

"Hey, sis. How are you?" Nate asked.

Natasha could tell he was being careful, weighing his words, feeling her out.

"I'm okay," she replied. "I ... uh, I wanted to apologize for last night. The fight, in front of your friends. It was stupid, and it shouldn't have happened. I'm sorry."

"Apology accepted. Where are you?"

"I'm at Avery and Jacob's," she explained. "I'm okay, I swear. And I really am sorry."

Nate sighed. "I appreciate the apology, Tash. The fight certainly has created quite the rumor mill around the bar, though."

"Great," she muttered. "Why does this feel like high school all over again?"

"Can I ask you a question, Tash?" her brother asked.

"I suppose," she said.

"What are your intentions with Mason?"

Natasha snorted. "What are you? His mother?"

"Natasha."

She froze at the tone of her brother's voice. He was serious.

"I ... I don't know. At first, I thought maybe we could be friends with benefits, you know? Then I thought maybe we could date, have fun, maybe see if it took off. Nothing serious, though. I wasn't ready for serious, or at least I didn't think I was ready for serious."

"Are you ready now?"

"I don't know," Natasha whispered. "Do you think I screwed everything up?"

"Maybe," Nate said. "You've known him for twenty years. Not only is he my best friend, but he's your friend, too. You didn't think some friends-with-benefits thing might affect that friendship?"

"I didn't think about that." She sighed. "Or maybe I did, but I ignored the potential shit show it could cause. I haven't exactly been thinking clearly lately."

"Can I ask you another question?" Nate said.

Despite the urge to say no, Natasha mumbled, "Yes."

"Did you really not know?" he asked.

"Know what?" she inquired, though she suspected she knew what Nate meant.

"You didn't know Mason was in love with you? All these years, everything he's done for you: being there time and time again, standing up for you, giving you a shoulder to cry on, all of it. You didn't know?"

Natasha sighed. This was the question she'd been asking herself all night. Had she known Mason was in love with her? Did she know it and choose to ignore it?

"Maybe I knew," she admitted. "But I think I ignored it. Because everyone kind of expected me and Mason to end up together, you know? You remember how Mom and Dad joked about it, and our friends thought it was funny to tease us and call us a couple? I so badly wanted to believe Mason was nothing more than a friend, so I ignored the hints I saw that showed he might want more. After a while, he was just Mason. If I needed a friend, I knew I could count on him. It never occurred to me he might read more into it."

"Even after you started to date?" Nate asked.

"No," Natasha snapped. "I didn't say that. The problem is, I didn't think. My heart led me, not my head. I was stupid."

"I'm going to sound like a broken record, but you need to talk to Mason. And you need to decide what you want from him. I know what he wants from you, and I think you do, too. Now you have to decide if you're willing to give him what he wants."

"You make it sound so easy," Natasha said.

"I know I do. And I also know it's difficult. Talk to him, Tasha. Don't leave this hanging between the two of you. You'll regret it if you do."

Natasha heard a faint crash through the phone, and then Nate cursed under his breath. "I gotta go. I hired a new server, and I think my glassware may be in trouble. If you need me, you know where to find me. I love you, sis."

"Love you too, Nathaniel." Natasha disconnected the call and tossed the phone on the bed. She leaned over, her head in her hands. Just thinking about talking to Mason made her stomach queasy. She threw herself back on the bed, one arm over her eyes.

Tomorrow. I'll talk to him tomorrow.

———

Tomorrow turned into two days and then three, and before Natasha knew it, it had been a week since she'd been home. Avery told her she could stay as long as she wanted. Even Jacob encouraged her to take her time deciding what she wanted to do.

She went back and forth to work and avoided the bar. She met Nate for lunch at Roselli's and got him to bring her some clothes. He was nice enough not to push her on the Mason issue. When she was at Avery and Jacob's, she hid in the bedroom, pretending to sleep when she was really moping. Work was her safe space; since the busy summer season had ended, the theater was empty all the time. She could hide out in her makeshift office at the back of the stage or pretend to clean the prop room or costume closet. Anything to avoid thinking about Mason.

Saturday night, she was in her office at the theater, supposedly finishing up paperwork when what she was really doing was reexamining the last twenty years of her life, going over every moment of time she'd spent with Mason. She realized at two in the morning how much she had ignored, intentionally and unintentionally.

Every time she broke up with one of her so-called boyfriends, Mason was there to pick up the pieces. He'd take her out for ice cream, order her favorite—chocolate with rainbow sprinkles—without even asking her what she wanted. Mason would listen to her talk, let her ramble on and on about the mess her life had become, and he never judged. He listened.

"Nat!"

Hearing her name being called in the empty theater made her jump. She shoved herself to her feet and stepped out of her office onto the black stage.

"Hello? Avery, is that you?"

"Where the hell are you?" Avery shouted. "It's so damn dark in here I can't see my hand in front of my face."

"Hold on!" Natasha took two steps to the right and hit the switch on the wall, illuminating the stage in the fluorescent light.

Avery stood at the bottom of the stairs leading to the stage, shielding her eyes with her hand.

Natasha smiled at her friend. "What are you doing here? It's late. I thought you'd be home by now."

"Jacob has a late class, so I thought I'd find you." She held up the plastic bag in her hand. "I stopped by the bar. Nate sent food; he said you probably hadn't eaten all day."

Natasha nodded. "He's right. Come on up. We'll eat in my office."

Avery hurried up the short set of stairs and across the stage. She ducked into the office and took a seat. "It's creepy in here when it's dark."

Natasha laughed. "I like it. I guess after spending so many years on stage, I'm used to it. The quiet of an empty theater is what I like the most. It lets me think."

Avery pulled food from the bag while Natasha grabbed waters and plastic utensils from a stash in the corner. "Oh, and how's that working for you?"

Natasha sighed as she sank into her squeaky office chair. "I don't know. I still don't know what to say to Mason. And every day that goes by makes it harder. He's going to think I don't care or that I don't want to fix this thing between us."

"Do you want to fix it?" Avery asked.

Natasha nibbled on a French fry and stared at a spot above Avery's head. "Yeah, I do. But it's weird, you know. Mason's supposedly in love with me, but sometimes I'm not even sure he knows me."

Avery narrowed her eyes. "I'm not so sure about that."

Natasha opened her mouth to protest, but Avery held up her hand. "Hear me out. Mason's always been around, right? I'd be willing to guess Mason knows you better than you know yourself."

"That's not possible," Natasha protested.

"Can I ask you a question?" Avery said. "Or maybe a couple of questions?"

"Yeah, of course."

"Does Brick know you don't like beer?"

"That's a weird question." Natasha snorted.

"Just answer it."

"Um, no, he doesn't. I guess I never told him I don't like beer."

"Okay," Avery continued, "does he know your favorite ice cream? Does Brick know you love baseball, but you don't like football? Does he know your favorite movie is *For the Love of the Game*? Does he know you didn't learn to drive until you were seventeen? Or that you've wanted to be an actress since you were a little girl? Does he know any of that stuff?"

Natasha swallowed the French fry that had turned to a lump in her mouth. "I ... I don't know. I don't think so. Why are you asking me these things?"

"Does Mason know?"

Natasha snorted. "Of course, he does. How could he not know? We've known each other forever."

Avery sat back and crossed her arms over her chest. "Nat, I haven't known you as long as Mason, but I know all that about you. I also know that you change when you date somebody. You try to mold yourself into someone you're not in order to please the guy you're with. You *act* like the girlfriend they want."

"I ... I do not." The words came out in a whisper, as if the words knew they weren't true even as they left her mouth. Natasha put her head in her hands and before she realized what was happening, her life and the boyfriends in it flashed through her head.

Reggie, her high school boyfriend: he wanted the beauty queen, the popular girl, the girl that made all the other guys envious. Natasha turned into exactly that, spending money on clothes, makeup, her hair and nails, anything to impress Reggie. He dumped her for a former girlfriend, the prom queen.

Mason picked up the pieces, reminding her that there was more to her than her looks.

Next up was Mike, a college sophomore, looking for the cute girl who was mature enough to deal with him. That lasted just a few months, even after Natasha did everything in her power to appear mature and sophisticated: ignoring her same-age friends, purging her room of her childhood memories, redecorating it into a sophisticated room fit for a college student. Mike broke up with her because she was too young.

Once again, Mason had been there, comforting her when she needed him most. He helped her unpack her stuffed animals and posters, even rehanging her favorites on her bedroom walls.

It had been the same with Dave and Bobby, guys who never really knew her, never appreciated her for her. Because she never showed them the real her. Natasha gave them what they wanted; she became the girl they wanted. And when those relationships were over, it was Mason she turned to for comfort.

Brick was the worst. His dislike of her twin brother and his jealousy of Mason—something she'd never understood until now—forced her to push both of them away. She'd hidden herself away in a dark depressing apartment, determined to make her relationship with the selfish jackass work; Natasha was sure she could make it work if she just tried harder to be what Brick wanted. In the end, it hadn't mattered what she did. Brick didn't love her and probably never had.

After finding Brick in bed with that co-ed, when she'd gone to her brother's looking for sanctuary, it had been Mason she'd really wanted to see. Because Mason would make it better.

Mason made everything better.

Over the last twenty years, she had ignored the one man in her life who would have given her the world. She kept him at arm's length and convinced herself that he was only a friend, nothing more.

Mason was always there whenever she needed him. For the longest time, she believed it was because of Nate, because he was her twin's best friend, and he was looking out for his best friend's sister. But the more she thought about it, the more she realized Mason was there because *she* needed him. It wasn't out of obligation to a friend or a misguided need to be the good guy; Mason looked out for her because he cared about her.

Because he loves me.

"Oh my god, Avery, I'm an idiot." Natasha brushed at the tears trickling down her face. "What have I done?"

Avery put her hand on her friend's arm and squeezed gently. "Nothing you can't fix."

"I have to go."

Natasha snatched her car keys off the desk and grabbed her backpack. She checked her watch. Hopefully, he was home.

Chapter 19

Mason

Mason hadn't seen Natasha in a week, not since the fight that had ended in the utter and complete devastation of his hopes and dreams. He'd done his best to distract himself: working long hours at the studio to facilitate the ownership change, and even picking up a couple extra EMT shifts, along with running every morning and sometimes late at night. He'd shove his earbuds in, playing his music at deafening levels in order to drown out his thoughts.

Tonight was no exception. He worked until almost nine before he headed home, ignoring Nate's texts suggesting he join him at the bar. Ten minutes after he got home, he was out the door again, the rhythmic pounding of his feet on the pavement in sync with the rhythm playing in his ears. The combination temporarily pushed all thoughts of Natasha and his screwed-up life out of his head.

Mason ran until his heart pounded, sweat ran down his face and chest, and his lungs were on fire. It was almost eleven when he unlocked the sliding glass door and stepped inside. Mason headed straight for the fridge; he needed water. The light barely illuminated the small room as he flipped it on over the kitchen sink. He grabbed a water, twisted off the top, and tossed it in the trash. Then he downed the entire bottle standing in the middle of the kitchen.

He unzipped his sweatshirt and yanked the earbuds from his ears before he tossed the empty bottle in the trash can at the end of the counter. He had only taken a couple of steps toward his room when he noticed her.

Natasha sat perched on the edge of the couch: head down, elbows on her knees, red hair hanging in her face. One of her legs bounced up and down, a nervous tic she had developed when she was anxious. She clasped her hands together between her legs, gripping each other so tight her knuckles were white.

Mason froze, stopping short of actually stepping from the kitchen into the living room, almost as if there were an invisible barrier between him and Natasha. She looked up, and they stared at each other from across the room, neither of them speaking. The tension was thick enough to cut with a knife.

"Hi," Mason said. He couldn't think of anything pithier than that. His brain froze along with his body.

"Hi," she replied. Natasha licked her lips and rubbed her hands together repeatedly, two other nervous habits she'd gained over the years. "I'm sorry if I startled you."

Mason took a step into the living room, just over the threshold from the kitchen. "I wasn't expecting you."

Natasha laughed, the sound hollow. "I almost didn't come in. I sat in the car for fifteen minutes talking myself into coming in here. Then I get inside, all set to talk to you, and you're not here. I almost left a dozen times."

He inched closer. "But you didn't."

"I should have. I wasn't sure you'd even talk to me." Natasha squirmed in her seat. "But Avery convinced me we needed to clear the air. Along with a few dozen phone calls from my brother."

"Okay, let's clear the air. You first." Mason nodded at her.

Natasha took a deep breath before speaking, then she let the words out in one long exhale. "I've behaved horribly. I've treated you horribly."

Mason shook his head before she even finished speaking. "It's okay—"

"No, it's not," she interrupted. "It's most definitely not okay. And I won't let you excuse my behavior, not anymore. I embarrassed us in front of all those people, some of them complete strangers. I can't believe we said those things to each other. We are two of the stupidest people on earth."

"I agree with that."

"Well, that's good." Natasha pushed herself off the couch and took two steps toward him. Her arms were crossed, hugging herself, protecting herself, and closing herself off because she felt vulnerable. He'd seen her do it dozens of times. She didn't look at him; instead, she stared at a spot on the floor between his shoes.

"I'm sorry," she whispered. "I freaked out. When I found out you had been in love with me for years, it screwed me up. I can't live up to the image of me you've created in your head. I'm not some woman to put on a pedestal and compare with every other woman on earth. I'm just me. I want someone who wants the real me, someone who sees the real Natasha Garin."

Mason shook his head, a smile teasing the corners of his mouth. "I know the real you, Natasha," he said. "I've seen you at your best, and I've seen you at your worst. I remember you in your unicorn t-shirt and bright purple shorts that you wore every day the summer after fifth grade. When you were so sick you had to sleep on the bathroom floor, covered in one of your grandmother's quilts, I was there. I've seen you falling down drunk and stone-cold sober. I know you can kick your brother's ass at Scrabble, but you let him win because it makes him feel good. You love chocolate ice cream with rainbow sprinkles, especially after a breakup. I know you had a pixie cut and braces in sixth grade."

Natasha blushed and shook her head. "Mason—"

"Let me finish." He closed the distance between them, cupped her cheek in his hand, and forced her to look up at him. "On prom night, you looked so gorgeous it made my heart stop. And when we graduated high school, you were all nervous and giggly, telling Nate you were going to call him Nathaniel because Nate sounded too immature." Mason took a deep breath, drinking Natasha in as she stared up at him. "You are the only woman I have seen for twenty years, even when I tried not to. I've seen you enough to know I am in love with you, Tasha. I love every single thing about you."

"Stop," Natasha murmured. A tear slid down her cheek.

Mason shook his head and slipped his arm around her waist. He pulled her flush against him and brushed a kiss across her lips.

"I can't. Not until you know that I'm in love with you. The real you. The woman you are when you're not pretending to be someone else. I don't need you to be something you're not because you are what I want."

Natasha grabbed the front of his hoodie and pulled in a breath so ragged, Mason felt it in his core.

"Say that again."

Mason rested his forehead on hers and closed his eyes. "I am in love with you. Since we were six years old, I have been in love with you. I love everything about you: all the good and all the crazy, even all the stuff that makes me insane. It doesn't matter because I love you. No matter what."

Natasha rested her cheek against his chest. "I always thought you and I would be friends forever. Even when we gave this dating thing a shot, I wasn't sure it would last. I didn't know what you wanted in a woman; I didn't know how to act to make you fall for me. I thought I had to act a certain way to get you to love me when all I had to do was be myself. I needed to stop pretending to be something I wasn't."

"And now?" Mason asked.

"I don't need to put on an act to earn your love," Natasha said. "I can be me."

"I want you to be you," Mason said. "That's all I ever wanted. *You*. Not a version of you that you create to make me love you. Just you."

Natasha nodded. "I can do that. I want to do that. I'm done pretending to be someone I'm not." She looked up at him, her eyes filled with tears. "I love you, Mace. I'm sorry it took me so long to realize it. But I love you."

Finally, after all these years, it felt as if a weight lifted from his shoulders with her proclamation. He slipped his hand into her hair and tilted her head back. The smile didn't leave his face even as his lips met hers. Her mouth opened to let him in, his tongue sliding against hers as their breath mingled and their bodies pressed together.

Mason lifted her up, her legs sliding around his waist while her arms were around his neck. The kiss deepened, the passion between them fueled by the years of denying their true feelings. Mason crossed the room in three long strides, hit the bedroom door with his shoulder, and stepped inside. His lips never left hers as he lowered her to the floor and kicked the door shut.

———

Mason rolled over, opened one eye, and checked the clock on the bedside table. Two a.m. Natasha slept soundly beside him, nothing visible but the top of her head, tendrils of red hair spread across the pillow. He eased out of bed, careful not to wake Natasha, pulled on his sweatpants and t-shirt, and slipped out of the bedroom. Nate sat on the couch with the TV on, sound down low, and the remote in his hand. He grinned at Mason.

"Hey, bro. Is that my sister's car outside?" Nate asked.

Mason nodded and pointed at his bedroom door over his shoulder. "Yeah. She's asleep."

Nate chuckled quietly. "Does that mean what I think it means? You guys made up?"

"We did," Mason said. He sat down on the opposite end of the couch. "I think we might be in a good place. Are you okay with that?"

Nate snorted. "Do you even have to ask? I'm definitely okay with it. Who wouldn't want their best friend dating their sister?"

"Just about every guy in the world." Mason chuckled. "But, seriously, you are okay with it, right? I don't want this to affect our friendship."

"It won't. If you hadn't fixed this whole thing," he gestured at Mason and the bedroom door, "that would have affected our friendship. This is a good thing. You and Tash belong together; you always have. I'm glad you finally figured it out." Nate put his hands on his knees and pushed himself off the couch. "Now, I'm off to bed. I thought you weren't ever going to come out of there. I've been waiting for over an hour."

Nate slapped his friend on the shoulder, muttered good night, and disappeared into his room. Mason shook his head and smiled. Hopefully, Nate's feelings wouldn't change.

Mason's bedroom door opened, and Natasha poked her head out the door. "Hey."

"Hi," Mason whispered. "I thought you were asleep?"

"I'm hungry. Do we have any ice cream?"

"I think so. What do you want? Chocolate with rainbow sprinkles?"

"Oh, no." Natasha laughed. "That's breakup ice cream. Do we have any vanilla and chocolate syrup?"

"I think we do," Mason said. "Why don't you go back to bed, and I'll get the ice cream?"

Natasha skipped across the room and put her hands on his shoulders. "Don't take too long." She kissed the corner of his mouth before spinning around and returning to the bedroom.

"Oh, I won't," Mason whispered at her departing form. "I'm not wasting another minute of my time with you."

THE END

Want to get all the latest info about Mimi Francis and her upcoming projects and events? Subscribe to her newsletter on mimifrancis.com for exclusive news, stories, and updates.

Book Club Questions:

1. Why do you think the author chose this particular book title? If you could pick a different title for the book, what would it be and why?

2. Do you think Natasha knew about Mason's feelings for her from the beginning?

3. What, if anything, did you dislike about Natasha? What did you dislike about Mason?

4. Should Mason have told Natasha how he felt about her years before? Would it have affected the outcome of their relationship?

5. Should Nate have intervened in the burgeoning relationship between his friend and his sister? Or was he right to let them figure it out?

6. Who was at fault for the fight? Natasha or Mason?

7. Would you forgive Natasha if you were Mason? Or vice versa?

8. Do you think Mason and Natasha were meant to be together?

Author Bio

Mimi Francis writes contemporary romance of the spicy, steamy variety. She loves writing tropes and frequently uses them in her series, Second Chances in Hollywood and Loves of Lakeside. Mimi ventured into writing when her favorite obsessions—Marvel and Supernatural—led her to writing fanfiction. With encouragement from friends, family, and her fanfiction readers, she successfully made the jump to writing original fiction.

When she's not writing, she works as an admin assistant, crochets, binge-watches her favorite TV shows and movies, and spends time with her three children, her dogs, and her husband.

www.ingramcontent.com/pod-product-compliance
Lightning Source LLC
Chambersburg PA
CBHW020149120726
47903CB00007B/2477